ASHES OF THE WIND

MADALYN RAE

CHAPTER 1

*T*hree months have passed, and I'm already sick of this shit. I didn't realize becoming the goddess of fire would also make me the chief person in charge of every whine and complaint in the fire elemental world. I flop down on the bright red couch in my bedroom suite with a deep sigh. In a day full of pointless meetings, this is the first time I've been alone and I'm relishing the silence.

A faint knock on the door draws me back to reality. "Yes?"

"I have your agenda for the evening," a familiar voice says.

Hell no. "Go away!" Guilt hits me instantly. "Murphy?"

"Aye," he answers.

"I didn't mean that, don't go away." I sigh, opening the door to see the man I love casually leaning against the door frame with his arms crossed.

"I know. May I come in?" Two dimples form on his cheeks, melting my anger slightly. The paper he's holding gets stuffed into his back pocket as he walks through the threshold. "We'll go over this later. I think cuddle time is more needed right now." He pulls me close, encasing me in my favorite place, the Murphy cocoon.

"This is why you're the perfect boyfriend. I'm sorry I'm being a bitch." He doesn't respond, instead, he holds me tighter.

"The past few months have been hard on everyone, you most of all. I can't imagine how you feel. Five months ago, you were a human trainer with no real clue about the elemental world. Now you've been thrown into the world of immortality full force." He steps back, keeping his hands on my shoulders.

"It's not the world that's exhausting, it's these damn fire elementals and all their drama. Llyr doesn't deal with drama with the water elementals. What the hell has Brigit been doing for the past century?" I pull away, falling dramatically on the couch.

Murphy sits on the opposite end, pulling my feet onto his lap. "It may not feel like it, but you've done a lot since being here. Brigit was preoccupied with killing everyone. To say she neglected her duties as goddess is a huge under-statement."

"What gave it away?" I motion to the space around me. "Have you taken time to look at this room and every-thing she left?" I jump up, walking toward a bookshelf still containing Brigit's belongings. "Just look how this place is decorated. At first glance it's nice, but when you really start to look at it, it's just..."

"Eccentric?"

"Exactly!" I choose a particularly ornate candlestick from the shelf. "Look at this thing." I turn it over in my hands. "It looks like it came straight from a production of 'Phantom of the Opera' and belongs on stage somewhere, not in my bedroom. And this," I pick up a wooden statue of a creature with one eye, a horn, and four legs. "What the hell is it?"

"Something we don't want to meet in person." He takes the statue and sets it back on the dresser.

"Are you saying that thing is real?"

"I don't know or want to know." He smiles. "We need to discuss a few things." I huff loudly, following him back to the couch as he pulls the paper out of his pocket. "The new chief of security is coming to dinner tonight, and the gala that follows will be in his honor."

"I would love a night off." I rub my hands along his chest. "*We* need a night off."

"Aye, we do." He pulls my hand to his lips, kissing each finger seductively. "But he'll be here before long and as a First Elemental and goddess of fire, your attendance will be expected." He continues kissing.

"If you keep doing that, I'm going to hold you captive, have my way with you, and neither of us will be in attendance tonight." I lace my fingers through his.

"Don't make promises we don't have time to keep," he flirts, moving closer.

A knock on the door interrupts. "What?" My tone is gruffer than intended.

"I have your dress for the evening, your highness." We sigh in unison.

"Come in," I call to the door, while Murphy puts space between us.

Rhys walks in, carrying a long garment bag. "Rhys, we've talked about this. Please call me Adria."

"Sorry, your high... I mean, Adria. I forgot." He hangs the dress on the wardrobe in the corner of the room. Flowing red taffeta explodes from the bag as soon as he unzips it.

"Oh, look... it's red." My voice is laced with sarcasm. Ever since becoming the goddess of fire, I've been surrounded by a rainbow of red hues. Red walls, red carpets, red ceilings, red clothing, red everything.

"Thank you, Rhys," Murphy dismisses the man who's willingly become my personal servant while being here. He smiles, flashing his amber eyes, and bows before leaving the room. Returning to the paper he brought with him, Murphy reads the schedule. "Cocktails will be at seven-thirty, followed by the meal at eight, and the gala at nine." He looks at the dress hanging on the front of the wardrobe. "As you can tell, the dress is black tie."

"Why can't you be the chief of security? I'm not a fan of bringing in an outsider." I prop my hands on my hips, trying not to act like a total brat.

"Aye, me either. But in this case, it's for the best. In this world, *I'm* technically the outsider, plus being a hybrid water elemental in a fire elemental world is a slight conflict of interest." He runs a hand through his auburn curls.

"You're the one bringing him here, and I trust you." I walk to the dress. "It just seems like all we've done since coming here is clean up Brigit's shit. I don't want any more issues."

"That's why we're bringing in fresh blood."

"Thank you," I mumble, mindlessly running my hands through the layers of taffeta. "Why is everything elementals do so formal? Why can't I wear sweatpants and a hoodie to meet this guy?"

"I am particular about some of the leggings and sweatpants you wear." He wiggles his eyebrows, relaxing me slightly. Since coming here, we haven't had five minutes alone or without interruption. I miss him, I miss us. "I'll be back in an hour to pick you up."

"Okay." I nod.

I take a quick shower, allowing the water to wash the stress and headaches of the day away. Truth is, I hate it here. After killing Brigit, the original goddess of fire, and her son Earwyn, I was forced to assume her role in the world of elementals and become the new goddess of fire, along with the official title of First Elemental. One out of ten, do not recommend.

The woman staring back at me in the mirror looks different. Blonde curls have grown longer since my transformation and my blue eyes, normally bright and full of energy, look dull and lackluster. Dark circles underneath give a sense of being sunken in. Fighting Brigit took a lot from me. More than anyone knows. The Adria that fought, died that day, leaving me a shell of what I once was. If it weren't for Murphy and the occasional visit from Shu, the god of air, and my grandfather, I would be lost in this world of fire and hideous red decor.

Growing up in the foster care system of California, I

never knew either of my parents. I didn't think it was possible to miss that life. Yes, it sucked, but at least it was mine. Here, everything I do is dictated to be for the good of Brigit's lessers *she* created centuries ago.

I turn on my favorite YouTube makeup guru and follow her glam tutorial. I'll be the center of attention tonight and need to look the part. "Suck up the pity party, Adria," I say to the image looking back at me. "You're the daughter of Llyr, the First Elemental of water, the granddaughter of Shu, the First Elemental of air, and the damn goddess and First Elemental of fire. Get over yourself and play the part you're meant to play." I rewind the video and follow her instructions until my face looks flawless. A fishtail braid and small ringlets on the side of my face complete the look. I look powerful and in control. Guess there is truth to the adage. Looks *can* be deceiving.

Sliding the dress over my head, I realize it's off the shoulder, and cut low enough I'll have to add two-sided tape to prevent a boob from escaping. Wearing this will certainly turn heads. Rhys outdid himself.

Being six feet tall, I usually choose low heels. Tonight, I want to appear larger than life itself. I choose three-inch silver rhinestone sandals that will make me the center of attention.

Murphy knocks as he opens the door. "Are you rea... shit."

"Is that a good shit, or bad shit?" I smile.

He closes the door behind him and moves closer, reminding me of a predator on the hunt. "Can we skip the event?" He slides his hands around each side of my waist.

"When I mentioned that earlier, it was a solid no from you. We've reached the point of no return."

"That was before you put on this dress." His grin is wicked, and I like it. "You look breathtaking. I mean, you always look beautiful, but... wow." Normally he's a half foot taller than me, but in these heels, we're close in height. He takes my hand, spinning me while whistling. "You're going to leave them speechless."

"Good. That'll be fewer people I have to talk to. Let's do this." He kisses my forehead, wrapping my arm through his, and we move into the long hallway that provides privacy from the rest of the castle.

"Tell me about this man." The dark hallway is the same color palette as the rest of the castle. Wall-to-wall dark burgundy carpet is surrounded by dreary brown walnut walls. Ornate Tiffany-style lamps hang every ten feet, casting dark shadows for our walk and giving the hallway a haunted house feel.

"Honestly, I don't know how I found him. His information kind of fell into my lap. I was surprised to discover he was local and comes with high accolades. His father was a fire elemental, and his mother's family has lived in Iceland for centuries." I stop.

"He's a hybrid? I thought he was a high-level lesser elemental?"

"I know what you're thinking and no, he never worked for Brigit, or was loyal to her. He went to school in California when he was eighteen and returned to Iceland a few weeks ago." He laces his fingers through mine.

"California? Really?" I'm excited to meet someone from my part of the world. "He can't be all bad then."

He kisses my fingers seductively, sending chill bumps up my arms. "Shall we go meet this boy from Cali?" He uses a horrific American accent.

"I think that would be a splendid, lovely idea," I answer in an equally horrible UK accent mashup.

He wraps my arm through his again, "Do me a favor?" I raise an eyebrow toward him. "Don't ever attempt that again. It was like a bad Lucky Charms commercial." He kisses me on the forehead.

I punch him in the shoulder with a laugh. "Bastard."

"Good evening, your highness." Rhys greets us. I give him a look. "I mean, Adria. Good evening, Adria." He stumbles over his words. "You look ravishing." He joins Murphy and me as we walk toward the ballroom.

"Thank you, Rhys. The dress is beautiful. Thank you for choosing it." His cheeks turn rosy. "Is our guest of honor here yet?" I ask, walking up a small flight of stairs that leads into the ballroom.

"He isn't, mistress. He sent word that he would be late to cocktails." He bows, moving back down the stairs.

"Ready?" Murphy asks. I take a deep breath, and the two of us enter the room full of people I'll have to talk to.

The crowd bows, practically in unison. "My queen, mistress, your highness," whispers are heard throughout the room.

"Thank you all for being here to support a new member of our family." I perform for the room of higher-level fire lessers staring at me. "Please, continue what you were doing." My words feel awkward. Where Brigit relished the fame, I despise it. The audience returns to their cocktails and conversations.

Murphy and I mingle through the room, greeting my fans, with me pretending to be someone I'm not. Most talk about Brigit, and how pleased they are with the change of leadership, others talk about the weather or their families. I try to look interested and entertained by each.

"Will you excuse me for a moment?" Murphy asks. "I need to check on our guest of honor." He kisses my hand, leaving me alone in the middle of the crowd. I continue greeting guests for the next few minutes until the need for fresh air overtakes me. Walking to the terrace that will lead to my escape, I shrink into the shadows, hoping to go unnoticed. The cool air that greets me is just what I needed. I take a deep breath, clearing my mind and soul.

"You alright, miss?" a deep voice asks. Shit. Back to performance mode. I turn, plastering on my fake smile and personality.

"Yes, I apologize. I was just getting some fresh air, the room felt quite... stuffy." I don't recognize the man standing in the doorway. He's as tall as Murphy with hair the color of coal and the signature amber-colored eyes all fire lessers share.

"I agree. I've been here all of two minutes and needed some air myself." He pulls a cigarette from a metal container. "Care for one?"

"No, thank you. I don't smoke."

"Mind if I do?" He slides the container into his coat pocket.

I wave to him. "Of course not," I lie.

He laughs softly. "I thought all fire elementals smoked." He takes a long drag on the cigarette, choking out a loud cough afterward.

"Been smoking for a long time, huh?" I hide my smile.

"A while," he answers, still coughing. "Which one of the stiffs in there is the new goddess of fire?" He nods to the ballroom. "I've heard she's a real pill."

I look up in question. "What have you heard?" I cross my arms.

He takes another drag on his cigarette, followed by a choking cough. "Not much, really. Just that she's come into the kingdom making a ton of changes. People are never a fan of change."

"No, I guess they're not." I don't know whether to laugh at his ignorance or egg him on.

The doors open as Murphy walks onto the terrace. "Ah, there you are. I see you've met Keegan." He slides an arm around my waist.

"Keegan? The new security chief?"

"Aye." He gestures toward my new cigarette-smoking friend. "Keegan Jacobson, may I present Adria Kane, goddess of fire." The cigarette falls from his mouth as he stands before me dumbfounded.

CHAPTER 2

*M*y wrist vibrates, waking me from what I hoped was a dream. Sadly, I'm met with red walls and carpet and realize it's all real. I roll over, finding my bed empty. Occasionally, Murphy will share my bed but not in the full sense of "sharing." We made the decision while with Llyr, not to go any further until we could fully commit ourselves to one another. At this point, I don't know if we've kept it that way because of our decision or the fact that we're under a constant spotlight and scrutiny since coming here. Either way and much to my dismay, our relationship has stayed relatively platonic.

I take my time getting dressed. I'm not in any hurry to hear the complaints of the day. Memories of Llyr and his castle fill my mind, making me homesick. He hasn't visited since I've been here, and I miss him. I missed out on twenty-three years with him, only to be separated again.

Murphy knocks before opening the door. "Good morning, sunshine." He hands me a cup of coffee.

"Oh, my gods. Is this what I think it is?" I caress the cup like he just handed me the holy grail.

"Aye, 'Murphy's Coffee and More' is back in business. The espresso machine finally came in. It takes forever for anything to be delivered here." He pulls the other hand from behind his back handing me a blueberry muffin. "I thought you might be hungry this morning."

Since becoming a First Elemental, my appetite has been nonexistent. I take the muffin, not wanting to seem ungrateful. Taking a sip from the coffee, the mocha hits every taste bud on the way down. "This is just as amazing as I remember."

"Good to see you still have an appetite for something." He kisses me on the forehead, taking the muffin back. "Ready to go?" he asks, eating half the muffin in one bite.

"I miss the days when we could train all day." I slip on a pair of low-heel dress boots that match perfectly with the tweed coat and slim-cut dress slacks I'm wearing.

"Aye, me too." He holds the door open for me. "I do have a bit of news you might like. I've set up a training session for you and Keegan this afternoon."

"Well, that should be fun. He can finish telling me all the gossip he's heard about me." I laugh. "He was just about to fill me in on everything before you came out last night."

Murphy stops walking. "What?"

"Keegan. Last night on the terrace. He didn't know who I was and asked which of the stiffs inside was the new goddess of fire. Said he'd heard she was a real pill."

He crosses his arms in front of his chest. "That arse."

"Truly, it was funny. Reminded me of life at the compound. For the first time since coming here, someone wasn't falling at my feet trying to impress me."

"I'll have a word with him." He moves toward the stairs.

"No, don't. I don't want it awkward between us. Besides, the look on his face when you introduced him to me was more than enough chastising." He stops, letting me go ahead of him.

"Good morning, Adria." Rhys greets me with a smile. His dark hair has flecks of white scattered throughout and his copper eyes have lost their intensity. He reaches a hand toward me, helping me down the last few steps.

"Good morning. You remembered to call me by my name." I smile. "What's in store for today?" I look around the unusually empty grand hall. Normally by this time of the day, at least ten higher-level fire lessers are waiting to meet with me about something I couldn't care less about. "Where is everyone?"

"You just have one meeting this morning." He leads me into the study that has become my office. "I believe this one will be more enjoyable than most." Llyr and Shu stand as I enter. Tears immediately fill my eyes.

"There she is," Shu says, holding his arms out for me. I rush to him, pulling him tight. "How have you been holding up?"

I fight the tears threatening to fall. "Shitty." I pull away, turning to my father. His eyes mirror mine. "Llyr?"

"I've missed you, girl." He kisses me on the forehead.

"I've missed you, too." I look between the two of

them. "What's going on?" Llyr steps back, keeping my hands held tightly in his. I'm not dumb enough to think the two of them have been hosting sleepovers and movie nights. Seeing them together sets off alarms. They share a look.

"We have some news," Shu announces, walking toward the bar cart in the corner.

"I'll be outside if you need me." Murphy follows Rhys to the door.

"Stay," Llyr interrupts. "This involves both of you." Rhys closes the door behind him.

"Ah, there you are," Shu talks to the brandy after locating and pouring a glass. "Anyone else care for a drink?" He raises his eyebrows in question.

"It's eight o'clock in the morning," Llyr answers, rolling his eyes.

"What's going on?" I repeat, looking between the two gods.

Llyr sighs before answering, "Astrid." Hearing her name fills me with dread. The last time anyone saw her was right before I killed her mother, Brigit, and brother, Earwyn, and assumed her role as goddess of fire. I'd imagine she's a little pissed at the moment, and I'm the target of her pissery.

"Has she been spotted? Is she close?" Questions fly out of my mouth in succession.

"Reconsidering that brandy now, aren't we?" Shu toasts the air in front of him.

"Let's sit down." Llyr leads me to the overstuffed couch. Murphy's still standing by the door, his arms crossed, and his face is unreadable. "She was spotted a week ago in Brazil."

I look at the faces of the men in the room. "Okay, and?"

Shu takes a sip of brandy before answering. "That's where Dagda lives."

I stand. "What am I missing? We knew they were together when she disappeared from the island. Or at least that's what you told me." No one will look me in the eye. "You're not telling me something."

"We lied," Shu admits, refilling his glass. "When the dust settled and the damage was assessed, she was gone and so was Dagda. Llyr," he toasts the air in the direction of the god of water, "just assumed they were together."

Murphy walks to my side. "How does this change anything? We thought they were together and now we know they are, why are we suddenly worried?" He slides a protective arm around my waist.

Llyr accepts the glass of brandy Shu is holding in the air, drinking it in one gulp. "Because they're not together anymore."

"I'm not following this conversation. Will someone just tell me what's going on?" My voice is full of frustration.

"Oh, good grief. Quit beating around the bush, Llyr." Shu slams his glass down. "We received word that Dagda is dead."

"The god of earth is dead? Only a child of a First Elemental can kill a First Elemental, right? You're the ones who told me that."

"We did," Llyr answers, raising an eyebrow.

"Astrid killed Dagda?" Murphy fills in the blanks.

"Ding, ding, ding! You get the gold star." Shu pours another glass.

I slide back on the couch. "That means..."

"That means she's now the goddess of earth and holds the power of fire in her blood." Llyr interrupts, copying Shu and filling his glass again.

"How's that possible? I'm the goddess of fire. Don't my powers trump hers or something?" I don't even know what I'm asking.

"She's the child of a First. As long as she has Brigit's blood flowing through her, she'll hold the power of fire." Llyr leans against the arm of the couch. "With the addition of earth, she's stronger than Shu and me."

"Meaning Adria's the only one strong enough to defeat her," Murphy finishes.

Shu clinks his glass against Llyr's. "Two gold stars for you! Told you he was a smart one."

I walk toward the duo. "What if we just leave each other alone? Each of us stays in our own lane?"

"If she was able to kill the god of earth, revenge is on her mind." Murphy stands. "Is that why you're here?" His voice sounds angry.

Llyr bows his head. "Yes."

I move to Murphy's side. "She's a child, for goodness sake. How can she be a threat?"

"She's a threat because she was raised in Brigit's household and trained from infancy to be an elemental killer. She's not like you, Adria. You were raised human, with a conscious and emotions. She was bred to do exactly what she's doing, kill. Don't let your ego get in the way of common sense. As you are right now, you don't stand a chance against her." For the first time since I've known him, Shu's angry. "You can barely control air. You have limited control of water and don't get me started on fire. My guess is you've been so damn busy putting out fires in this hell hole, pun *fully* intended, that you haven't had one minute to learn how to control the element. It's time to embrace who you are, Adria. Be the warrior you were born to be."

I sit down in defeat. He's right. Dammit, he's right. "What do I need to do?"

Llyr sits beside me. "You have to accept who you are."

"That's the problem. I don't know who I am!" I wipe a tear from my cheek.

"That's where you're wrong," he answers. "You know, you just haven't accepted it." I lay my head on his shoulder. "You grew up in the mundane world. This world of magic, elementals, and powers beyond comprehension were stories for movies, fairytales, and fantasy books, not real life. Part of you still thinks that way. Until you release the human part of you and embrace who you truly are, your powers won't fully be yours."

"What if I don't want to give that part of me up?"

"Then you'll never be strong enough." He pulls me close to his side.

"What's to keep her from coming after one of you?" Murphy asks, unlocking a new fear.

Shu sets his glass down. "Don't worry about Llyr and

me. We have a little bit of experience on the young sparkling. We'll be fine, we always are. We'll come out smelling like a rose."

Llyr continues, "You're her target. Her emotions are raw when it comes to you. You're responsible for her brother's and mother's deaths. She'll have vengeance on the top of her list."

"You're saying Adria needs to train and be ready for what's coming?" Murphy asks.

Llyr stands. "No, she needs to do more than train. She needs to lose the part of her that's holding her back and accept her destiny. That's the only way Astrid can be defeated."

"Forgive my boldness, your highnesses, but this is bull-shit." Murphy walks toward a window overlooking the mountains. Curls turn to frizz as he runs his hands through them. "You two sent her into this world blind. Now you show up, months later to tell her that she has to let go of her human self, the only part she has remaining of herself, and become fully elemental, just so she can kill a crazed teenager who has vengeance on her mind? Am I missing anything?"

"No, I think that covers it." Shu takes another drink.

"You're forgetting that crazed teenager is the goddess of earth and fire." Llyr's anger matches Murphy's. "She wasn't, nor ever will be, human, in any sense of the word. Her human father was nothing more than a sperm donor, most likely killed after doing his part." He walks back to me. "I'm sorry, Adria. I know this is overwhelming and I wish there was an easy solution, but there's not. She's going to come after you and there's nothing I can do to prevent it."

I stand from the couch, moving away from them all. "Murphy's right, this is bullshit." Murphy takes a step toward me. "No, stay where you are. I need to say this." I take a deep breath, trying to regulate the intensity of the words I want to scream. I look Llyr in the eyes. "I never asked for any of this. My life was sucky, but it was mine. I controlled when I woke up, who I talked to, and where I went. The moment Murphy walked into that compound, everything changed." Murphy looks down at my words. "Shit, I'm not sure how to say what I want to say."

"Just speak your mind, girl," Shu answers. "You've earned it."

I sigh loudly. "Growing up human may seem like a weakness to you all, but it wasn't. It made me strong and made me who I am today. I had to fight for every damn thing and yes, at the time I hated it. But now, I realize it was a blessing. It's what gave me the ability to know what I'm capable of. Why do I have to let go of that part of me to defeat Astrid? It's like asking me to give up my left arm because my right arm is stronger. Aren't I stronger with both arms?" The three of them stare at me, not sure what to say.

"Don't ask me to give up what makes me, me." Instead of letting tears fall, I stand tall, pulling my shoulders back and looking each of them in the eye. "You two," I say, looking between Llyr and Shu, "fell in love with human women. If not, I wouldn't be here." Both look down. "If my humanity makes me weak, then I'm not alone in that endeavor. It seems to have made the two of you weak as well."

"I'm not sure *love* is the word," Shu corrects. Llyr sends him a warning look. "What?" Shu shrugs, finishing off the last of the brandy.

"I'm not going to sit here and wait for Astrid to find me, but I'm not going looking either. I'll train, but you can't ask me to give up what's left of me." I wrap my arms around my chest.

Llyr moves closer. "You amaze me, daughter." His large hand slides along my cheek. "You have so much of your mother in you. I see it more and more each time we're together. Asking you to lose that part of you is like losing Claire all over again. You're right. There has to be another way, and we'll find it." I wrap my arms around his waist, burying my head in his chest. "We'll figure this out, together."

"You need more brandy," Shu announces, shaking an empty carafe and lightening the mood and heavy energy in the room slightly.

"I'll get right on that." I pull away.

"Also, can we do something about this gods awful decor?" He looks around the study. "It's so Gothic and dark in here. It's giving me B-list horror movie vibes."

"The red is hideous," I answer.

"Yes! Let's fix that." He pulls a MacBook out of a bag I didn't realize he was carrying. "Retail therapy can fix just about anything."

"Now who sounds human?" I laugh. Shu pats the seat beside him on the couch where he's already searching Pinterest for ideas on decorating a castle.

Shu and I spend the rest of the morning making choice boards for my bedroom suite, the study, and the dining room, while Llyr and Murphy discuss training strategies. "Let me know when the items start coming in and I'll zap right in to help decorate." Shu closes his computer. "I live for design."

"Thank you." I wrap my arm around his thin waist. "You were right. Retail therapy was very therapeutic."

He kisses me on the forehead. "My pleasure, my dear. Don't worry, everything is going to be okay." He looks over at Murphy and Llyr, who have given up talk of the future and are playing a game of chess. Each staring silently at the board. "Those two are more alike than they want to admit."

I huff a laugh. "Maybe they are."

"Don't worry about Astrid. It's going to be a while before she's ready to do much of anything except sleep. You remember those days." He slides a backpack over his shoulder.

The months after killing Brigit were spent floating in between the void and reality. "I do. Too bad we can't just find her body and kill her before she ascends into her power."

"Believe me, we've tried," Llyr answers. "South America is a large continent. Wherever she is, she's well protected."

"That gives us enough time to figure this out and change this place from a dungeon to a castle. I wonder if one of those television shows could film a special here?" He walks toward the chess game, moving Llyr's king. "Oops, check mate."

"What the hell, Shu?" Llyr asks, making me laugh.

"It's time to go," Shu answers.

Llyr wraps his arms around my shoulders. "It's going to be okay. I promise."

"Don't make promises you don't know if you can keep." He doesn't respond, instead, the two of them pop out of existence, together.

CHAPTER 3

"*A*re there any more meetings this afternoon?" Murphy whispers as the last group leaves the office. "I'm tired of hearing complaints."

"What? You're not enjoying hearing about family disputes that have nothing to do with anything important?" I sigh, leaning back in the leather desk chair.

He stretches his long legs in front of him. "With the risk of sounding like a complete jerk... no."

"Agreed. Let's go." I stand, pulling him with me.

"You don't have to tell me twice."

Rhys is waiting next to the door with our next meeting participants. "Adria, your next meeting is ready." Two older men stand, ready to enter.

"Gentleman, you'll have to excuse me, but I'm going to need to reschedule." The men bow, murmuring their disappointments. "Rhys, please reschedule the rest of this week's meetings and send my apologies."

"Yes, ma'am." He stumbles over his words.

Murphy follows me to our quarters. "What do you have in mind?" He backs me up to the doorway of my room.

"I need to get out of this place. I want to run like we used to." I reach up, kissing him on the lips, soft with a promise of more. He doesn't waste a minute to return the gesture, pulling me closer.

"I have a better idea," he pants, between kisses. Gods, his lips feel amazing against mine. The swish of his tongue jolts my senses, helping me realize how badly I've missed this, missed him.

"Your idea is better than mine." Murphy presses his body into mine. Evidence of his arousal presses against my abdomen, lighting my body on fire. He deepens our kiss as his hand grips my butt sending sensations of pleasure through my body.

Rhys clears his throat a few feet away from our frenzy. "Excuse me, your highness." Murphy stops kissing me, backing away to a respectable distance, taking the fire of our connection with him. I don't remember a moment ever feeling this awkward.

I plaster on a fake smile while wiping lip gloss off my chin. "Yes?"

"Please forgive my intrusion. I wouldn't have disturbed you if..."

"What do you need?" I interrupt his apology.

Rhys shifts from foot to foot. "Mr. Jacobson is waiting downstairs for training. He says the two of you had a pre-scheduled appointment for this afternoon."

"Shit," Murphy whispers. "I forgot about him."

I clear my throat. "We were just about to go for a run. Please tell Mr. Jacobson we'll meet him in ten minutes."

"Yes ma'am." He turns.

"Rhys," I call after him. "Tell him to make sure he's dressed for a run." He nods, turning back toward the stairs.

"That was awkward," Murphy says with a smile. "Looks like we're going for a run after all."

"It does." I kiss him quickly on the cheek. "Meet you back out here?"

He sighs and bows. "Yes, your highness." I send a blast of water straight into his shoulder.

"Now my shirt's wet. I'll just have to take it off." He reaches slowly above his head, peeling the soaked shirt from his chiseled torso. His moves are slow and calculated, making me reconsider our run. Reaching behind me, I turn the doorknob to my room and slide through the threshold backward.

"Five minutes," I say, closing the door on my private striptease. Over the months, I've replaced a lot of my clothing that was damaged when I destroyed the castle in the UK, but my choice of workout clothes is limited. I choose a pair of leggings and a tank top that are flattering, yet non-hoish. Surprisingly, a difficult task. Murphy returns to my door just as I finish tying my last shoestring.

"I was too slow." His words are flirty as he crosses his arms across his chest.

"Yes, you are. I stood naked in the middle of the room waiting, but you never came back. I gave up and dressed." He laughs loudly.

"Good thing Rhys didn't show up for that."

"Can you imagine?" I slide my hand down the side of his butt as I walk into the hallway. "Ready?"

His laugh is low and sexy. "No."

"Too bad." I grab his hand, pulling him out of the room.

Keegan's waiting at the bottom of the stairs. He's wearing a pair of too-short shorts, a tank top, and a terrycloth headband. Murphy snickers, "Who dressed him?"

"Nineteen eighty-six," I answer, holding in a smile.

Keegan drops to his knees. "Your Highness." He resembles a knight, bowing to a king.

"That's not necessary. I'm just Adria." He stands to full height, bringing him and Murphy even.

"I want to apologize for my behavior last night. I was rude and out of line..." I hold up a hand, interrupting his apology.

"Keegan, your apology isn't necessary. Honestly, it was nice to not have someone walking on eggshells around me. However, I hope once you get to know me, your opinion will change." I smile warmly, hoping to reassure him. "Murphy and I were just about to go for a run. Care to join us?"

"I'm not much of a runner, but I'd be honored." He follows us through the door.

"Maybe you can share some history of this beautiful land as we run." I haven't run in so long, stretching out is painful.

"Of course," he answers.

This is the first time I've left the castle grounds since arriving in Iceland and it feels wonderful. The faint smell of the sea hits my nose, relaxing me instantly. Where Llyr's castle is part of the village, this one is miles away from humans and their lives. We top a small crest and a village sits in the valley below. "That's where I'm from," Keegan says proudly.

The scene looks straight from a postcard. "It's beautiful," I whisper. A tall steeple is the highest point in the valley. Houses line a narrow street, leading to the front of the church, branching off into several smaller, house-lined roads. "How many people live there?"

"When I left, there were around eighty families. Probably a few more than that now."

"Reminds me of home." Murphy crosses his arms over his chest.

Behind the village, snow-covered mountains loom in the distance. "Does snow stay on those mountains all year?"

"Yes. It never gets above freezing up there." He points to a taller mountain in the back. "See that big one?"

"Yes," Murphy and I answer in unison.

"That's a volcano."

"No shit?" Murphy's tone sounds boyish.

"Not one single shit." Keegan laughs.

Such a beautiful killer. "Has it ever..."

"Erupted?" Keegan interrupts. "Not in the last fifteen hundred years."

Murphy looks like a kid in a candy shop. "Was there a village here when it erupted?"

"Yes, both the village and its inhabitants were destroyed."

"Hard to believe something that beautiful can wipe

out all existence with one explosion," I say in awe. Murphy's expression changes. Without asking, I know what he's thinking. The irony isn't lost on me. I'm just as capable as the volcano when it comes to destroying everything around me.

"The sea looks so clear." Murphy points to the dark blue expanse not far to the left of the village. "Why don't we go for a visit?" He takes off running, while Keegan and I follow behind. The closer we get, the clearer my head becomes.

"Why have we waited this long to explore?" I ask Murphy.

"I don't know, but I'm glad we didn't wait another minute. I've passed it a few times on the way to the village but never had the chance to stop." The three of us approach the cliff overlooking the sea. Keegan looks nervous, staying a few feet behind Murphy and me. "What I wouldn't give for a swim." Murphy closes his eyes.

"That first step's a doozy." Keegan laughs "You might need to master the art of flying before you attempt it." His words light an invisible lightbulb trapped in my brain.

I reach for Murphy's hand, and he smiles knowingly. "Keegan, take my hand."

"Your Highness?" he asks.

"Keegan, I'm not flirting with you. Take my hand, oh, and you might want to close your eyes." He takes my hand but keeps his eyes open. "Your call." I smile. "Air," whispers from my lips as the three of us are lifted off the edge and down to the small sandy beach below.

"Holy shit!" Keegan exclaims. "What the hell was that? Did we just fly?"

"It's more like moving energy," Murphy answers, using my description. "It gets easier the more you do it." He laughs, wrapping his arm around my shoulders. "Thank you. This is exactly what I, what we, needed." The two of us breathe deeply, taking the salty air deep into our lungs.

"You two like this, huh?" Keegan asks. "Water has never been a favorite of mine."

"Aye, I can imagine being a fire hybrid might have something to do with that." Murphy lays his head on top of mine, kicking the dark sand beneath his foot. "Why's the sand black? I've never seen it this color."

"That's due to our friend over there." He points to the volcano. "After the last eruption, the lava mixed with the sea, turning it black and eventually breaking down into sand."

"It's beautiful." I take a scoop into my hand, letting it fall between my fingers. "Too bad the water's freezing. I could use a swim." I swirl my hand through the blue hue. When the water touches my skin, what resembles snowflakes form on my skin. "Hello, my friends," I whisper to the elementals below. Several moments pass before a whisper returns. "Hello, my queen." I recognize the tone as being the water elemental I first met at the compound in California. "Did you hear that?" I ask Murphy.

"Aye, I did." Tears form in my eyes.

"What's his name?"

"Tempest," he answers with a smile.

"Can he form into anything besides water? I mean, could he physically come to the castle?"

His smile is infectious. "Aye, he can. He was responsible for training me when I first came to the castle on the Isle." His hair frizzes as he runs a hand through his auburn curls. "He's kind of temperamental though. You'll have to ask him yourself about visiting the castle."

"That's the pot calling the kettle," a deep voice rumbles through my mind. I turn to see Murphy smiling ear to ear.

"Did you just hear someone speak in your mind? Am I crazy?"

"Forgive me, your highness. I didn't mean to frighten you. The wee one is right. My name is Tempest and I'm responsible for his training. The good parts, at least."

His words warm my heart. "How do I talk to him?" I ask Murphy.

"Like you have been, or in your head. Just direct the words to him." He turns toward the sea, seemingly speaking to his friend.

"Are you talking to him now?"

"Aye, I did."

"Why can't I hear your words in my mind?" I'm confused about how this is the first time I've heard a water elemental speak through my mind.

"Because I'm a hybrid." His answer is simple and short. "Tempest can speak to you, as he has before, but he's limited while in elemental form. Through telepathy, he can carry on a fluid conversation." He turns to the water, saying something I can't hear.

"I'm good at conversation," Tempest retorts. *"Especially when it's something important."* His voice sounds in my mind.

"Tempest?" I call to the sea, using my mind.

A small swirl forms into a ten-foot-tall wall of water, complete with arms, legs, and a head. He bows, "My queen," echoes off the cliff wall behind me.

Seeing him standing there, chill bumps cover my skin, head to toe. I return the gesture, bowing to him. "My friend," I whisper. "Thank you for being here."

"I would have it no other way," he whispers in my mind. *"You are my queen and I will protect you with my life."*

Keegan looks terrified, facing the large creature. *"One day, I would like you to visit the castle. Is that something you would be able to do?"* Tempest pauses before answering.

"It would be my honor, my queen." He bows again and I can't hide my smile. *"Until that day, I will be here, protecting you and your waters with my life."*

"Until then," I answer out loud. "Thank you, Tempest." I watch as the wall disappears into the sea, leaving us alone on the beach.

"Holy shit!" Keegan says. "Did a wall of water just carry on a conversation with you?"

"He did." I wrap both arms around Murphy's waist. "Why did that make me emotional?"

"Because he feels like home." Murphy pulls me tight.

"I hate to interrupt whatever's going on over there, but I think I'd like to be back on the cliff now." Keegan's voice sounds shaky.

"Okay." I laugh. "Air," I whisper, and the three of us return to the top, overlooking the sea. "This is exactly what I needed." Taking a deep breath, I take in as much *home* as possible.

"Aye," Murphy agrees.

"I have more to show you, but I've made a mental note to stay away from cliffs." Keegan begins jogging toward the small village. We follow behind.

The road leading to the village is narrow and winding. Clearly built before the age of automobiles. We enter the village, stopping beside the church that looked so small from above. From here, the steeple appears endless.

"This is the village I grew up in," he says, giving us the 'five-dollar tour,' as he called it. The homes and buildings are painted brightly, which is accented by the deep green grass and bright blue sky. The colors appear brighter than anywhere I've been before.

He leads us into a small storefront lining the main road. "This is where I worked and lived before going to California." The inside of the store reminds me of internet pictures of diners from the '50s. A long bar with cushioned barstools lines one side of the store, while on the opposite are display cases full of every kind of chocolate and candy known to man.

"Look who it is!" An older, grey-haired woman walks around the side of the bar. "Keegan!" She stops. "What are you wearing?"

Keegan smiles, hugging the woman. "It was all I could find to run in." She laughs, looking him up and down. "Brenna, this is Murphy and Adria. I'm giving them a tour of the village. Everyone knows no tour is complete without one of your homemade milkshakes."

She motions to the stools in front. "Here, sit down. It's my treat." Before we have a chance to respond, she's behind the counter scooping homemade deliciousness into large silver cups. "Don't tell me what you want. I'm going to guess. It's my superpower." Her energy is kind and warm, and I mirror the same back to her. She sets the first glass in front of me. "For the beautiful lady, I made my specialty. I call it Oceans Alive." Aqua blue ice cream shows through the clear glass. I take a sip and close my eyes at the perfection of her creation.

"This is the best milkshake I've ever had." I smile.

"It'd better be!" She pats my hand before turning to make two more. "For this handsome guy, another of my creations. She sets a glass full of green ice cream in front of him. "I call this one the Stud Muffin." I choke at her words. Murphy takes a huge gulp, and his eyes grow large.

"This is amazing. Thank you."

"Oh, my. He's tall, red-headed, and has an accent." She turns to me. "Hold on to this one, girl."

I smile at Murphy. "I plan to." He reaches over, lacing his fingers through mine as we sip our milkshakes together.

"Your usual, Keegan?"

"Please!" he answers with the excitement of a small child. Not a minute later, a red milkshake is set in front of him. He barely waits for her to set it down before taking a huge gulp. "This is exactly as I remember." He closes his eyes in bliss. Thank you, you're one in a million."

"Aww, I don't know about all that. I don't get too many new faces around here. It's good to meet new people and give them a special treat." She wipes the remaining ice cream off her hands, sitting on a stool opposite us. "What brings you two to our humble little village?"

"We're living at the castle not far from here."

Brenna raises her eyebrows in surprise. "Is that so?" She wipes the counter, clearing it of invisible droplets.

"Yes, ma'am," Murphy answers.

She and Keegan exchange a look. "I haven't been to that castle in years. Not a place for happy memories. Can I offer you three some freshly made chocolate before you leave?" She's on the other side of the store before I realized she moved.

"No, thank you," I answer.

"I'd love some chocolate-covered orange slices," Murphy says, surprising me. What the hell's a chocolate-covered orange slice?

"You're in luck, my red-headed friend. I made some fresh ones this morning. Dark or milk chocolate?" She opens the candy door.

"Dark, please."

"I knew I liked you." She picks several large slices of strange-looking candy out of the cabinet. "Dark chocolate is the only way to eat 'em." She fills a bag full, making Murphy smile ear to ear. He pulls out his wallet to pay. "No, they're on the house." She waves his money away. "It's been a pleasure to talk to new people. Anytime you're in town, please stop by and say hello." She walks around the counter, handing Murphy a bag of what looks like chocolate turds.

"Thank you, Brenna," I say, walking to the door. "It's been a pleasure to meet you. Your milkshake creation isn't something I'll soon forget."

"You're welcome, dearie. Come visit anytime you feel like." She turns to Keegan. "Take care of yourself, boy."

She gives him a quick hug and opens the door for us, patting Murphy and me on the shoulder as we leave.

"Are all humans in this village as friendly as she is?" I ask, waving again to the woman staring out the windows.

"Pretty much," Keegan answers. He turns, blowing a kiss to our ice cream barista. "Brenna raised me after my elemental father skipped town and my mother died. Before then, I lived with my grandmother who thought of me as an abomination. She became the parent I never had."

"Your childhood has a familiar ring to it." The sun is beginning to set, bringing a warm glow through the peaks of the mountains. We run in silence as the castle comes into view. In Iceland, the sun stays in this same position until close to midnight when it finally sets for a few hours.

I immediately notice flames and smoke rising from the back of the castle grounds the closer we get. "What's that?" I pick up speed.

"Looks like there's a fire." We take off in a full sprint toward the castle. Entering the courtyard, I see Rhys and several of the kitchen staff trying to put the flames out with a water hose.

"Air." I raise off the ground, moving above the roaring fire. Calling on the part of me that's the strongest, I hit the flames with a wall of water, immediately extinguishing them before lowering to the ground.

"What happened?" I demand.

"I don't know, your highness." I don't bother correcting him. "I saw the flames from the office window. One minute there was nothing, the next they were there." I look around the circle of fire elementals, any of which are capable of starting a simple grass fire. Did one of them do this? Was this a warning from Astrid?

"Thank you, Rhys." I make eye contact with each of the lessers. "Thank you, all." One by one, they bow their heads and return to their duties in the castle. "Rhys," I call after him. "Is there anything I should know?"

"No, ma'am. It started only a few minutes before you arrived."

I watch him walk inside. "Looks like you have your first mission, Keegan."

"Yes, ma'am. I'll work on that now." He moves toward the door.

"No, tomorrow. Get some rest. We'll be safe for the night."

He nods, "Tomorrow then. Good night."

......

Back in the privacy of my room, Murphy sits on the hideous couch and pulls me into his lap. The warmth of our connections fills me with energy. "Do you think someone on the castle grounds started the fire, or could it have been..."

"It wasn't Astrid," he interrupts. "She'll be still recovering from assuming Dagda's element. There's no way she's reborn and here already."

"Maybe it wasn't her, but one of her cronies." I snuggle closer.

"Let's see what Keegan discovers. It'll be his first assignment and will give me a chance to assess his skills." Murphy pulls me tight.

"I like him," I whisper.

"Looks like I need to fire him." He laughs.

"Not like that. But I like him." I pause. "There's definitely more to his story than he's telling, but he has a calm energy and is honest."

"That reminds me." He pulls the scrunched-up bag of chocolate from his pocket, shoving one of the turd-looking slices into his mouth. "Oh, my gods. This is the best thing I've eaten in a long time." He sits back, relishing the joy of his disgusting treat. "You're right. He's definitely keeping secrets."

"Don't we all?" I rest my head on his chest.

CHAPTER 4

J wake to the familiar buzz on my wrist. Murphy's lengthways across the couch, and I'm somehow squeezed between him and the cushions. From the sound of his breathing, he's still sleeping or possibly in a chocolate-induced coma. The bag of orange slices sits on his chest, half empty. I spider-monkey my way off the couch without disturbing him and head to the bathroom. One look in the mirror tells me it's hair-washing day. Brushing through the tangles of yesterday, a movement behind me catches my attention. I turn, finding nothing. Out of the corner of my eye, I see it again. *What the hell?*

"Hello?" I call into my closet. "Is someone here?" The red dress I wore to the gala swings.

"It's just me," Hannah says, walking through the second closet door. "Geez, when'd you get so jumpy?"

"Oh, my gods. Hannah! It's been months since you've visited!" I hug my dead best friend. The top of her head barely reaches my shoulders. "I was beginning to think you weren't coming back." She's wearing the torn blue jeans and alien hoodie from her last visit.

"I'm always with you, whether you need me or not." She flashes a smile.

"I'll always need you."

She pulls a red Twizzler from the hoodie pocket. "Then I guess you're stuck with me." She looks me up and down. "What's going on with your hair? What's the look we're going for?"

I choke back a laugh. "It's called, sleeping squished between a giant and the back of the sofa. Like it?"

"Eh, I've seen worse." She explores the closet, running her hands through the rows of clothing. "Looks like you're getting more clothes."

"I guess. I haven't really had time to shop. Too much shit to deal with here." I slide my butt on top of the bathroom vanity. "This goddess thing isn't as glamourous as you'd think."

"These are super cute!" She straps on a pair of turquoise Converse high-tops that resemble clown shoes on her tiny feet. "Dammit, they're too big."

"Hannah, I don't know what I'm doing," I confess.

"Sure, you do. Just be you." She's switched from the Converse to a pair of three-inch heels.

"Astrid killed Dagda."

"I know." She struggles to walk through the closet without falling. "She's acclimated to his element quickly."

"What are you saying?"

"She's already assumed Dagda's element. She's no longer 'sleeping.'" She holds up quotation mark fingers.

I slide off the vanity. "Are you sure? Shu said it would take at least six months."

She's suddenly standing directly in front of me. "I'm sure. That's why I've come. Shu and Llyr were wrong about the timeline, but right about her intentions. She has this kingdom and your powers in her sights."

"What if she goes after *them* first?" Hannah knows what I'm asking.

"Shu and Llyr have a millennium of knowing how to stay hidden and safe. You don't. Why go after them separately when she can come after you with the same results?" Hannah's playful nature has changed to serious in an instant.

"What?"

"It's easier to kill one First Elemental and assume their power than kill two." She disappears.

"Hannah?" I whisper into the emptiness. Dammit, she's right, and deep inside I've known all along she was out there. I adjust the temperature of the shower and let the water clear my mind. Thoughts of Hannah's conversation, of our run yesterday, and of my life since stepping into this role run through my mind in rapid succession. In a moment of clarity, I know what I have to do.

Five minutes later, I'm standing in front of a still-sleeping giant, gently rubbing his stubbled chin. He takes a deep breath, "Good morning, sunshine." He rubs a hand through his frizzy curls. "You're a sight for sore eyes." He pulls me on top of him, squishing the bag of chocolate between us. "That's going to leave a stain." A smile sounds through his voice.

"I need to learn how to control fire," I whisper into his chest. "I don't want to wait any longer."

He sits up, taking me with him. "Did something happen?" I've never told him about Hannah. It's always seemed like something personal, something for me alone.

"Nothing other than what Shu and Llyr told us." I move away from the couch. "Astrid's going to come after me sooner, than later. I need to know how to control fire. I have the power of three elements, but don't know how to fully control any of them."

"Okay," he agrees. "I'll do some checking around to find someone who I trust to work with you."

"I already know who."

He looks up in question. "Rhys? He's a nice guy, but I don't see him as your teacher."

"Keegan," I answer.

Murphy wrinkles his forehead. "He's a hybrid. He won't have control of his element."

"You do," I retort.

"Aye, but I'm special." He stands, making the bag of chocolate fall to the floor. "Well, shit." He scoops them back into the bag. "What is it Americans say? Three-second rule?"

"Something like that." I smile. "I sense Keegan's power. He's strong and I'm willing to bet he can control his element."

He licks the chocolate off his fingers. "What exactly do you sense?"

"He's as strong as you." Murphy looks offended. I wrap my arms around his narrow waist. "I trust him."

······

An hour and pretending to eat breakfast later, Keegan walks into the office dressed in an outfit similar to yesterday. "Your Highness," he says, with a bow.

"Seriously?" I stand. "Please call me Adria. And for gods sake, don't bow to me."

Keegan stands, clearing his throat awkwardly. "You wanted to see me?" I step around the desk, moving in front of him.

"I want you to train me."

"Sounds like a plan. That's why I wore my jogging clothes." He pulls the sweatband away from his forehead, letting it pop back in place.

"Is that what those are? Jogging clothes?" I try not to smile as he looks down at the booty shorts he's wearing. "I don't want you to train me physically. I've got that covered. I want you to teach me how to control fire."

Keegan stares at me blankly. "I don't know how to do that."

I move closer. "I think you do."

"I'm a hybrid, not a lesser." He raises his eyebrows in question. "Hybrids can't control their element."

I lean against the edge of my desk. "Most can't, but I think *you* can." Keegan doesn't answer. "I sense it in you." I open the double doors. "Rhys, please ask Murphy to join us."

Several minutes pass before Murphy walks through the doors. "You rang?"

"Would you mind showing Keegan what you can do?" Keegan looks anxious as Murphy hands him an empty brandy glass and moves to the back of the room. A stream of water fills Keegan's glass to the brim.

"What the hell?" He drops the glass on the carpet. "Where did that come from?" Murphy smiles and waves from the corner. Keegan looks completely confused. "You expect me to believe *you* did that. No way, dude."

"Aye, 'twas me."

Keegan picks up the now empty glass. "Do it again. This time, Adria looks away." I turn toward the window as Murphy fills the glass a second time. Keegan carefully sets the glass on the table without speaking.

"I know how you feel," Murphy says. "I kept my abilities hidden for years." He looks at me. "You can trust us. If Adria senses power in you, she's not wrong."

Keegan walks to a window on the other side of the room. "I've never met a hybrid with abilities. A normal one, at least."

"Aye, me either."

"Keegan, I need to be trained, and I want you to do it," I repeat.

"Why not one of the high-level lessers? There are plenty around here who would jump at the chance to train the goddess of fire."

"Because that same sense that tells me you hold the power of fire is the same sense that tells me you're someone I can trust." I give him time to process my words.

"What if you're wrong?" he asks.

I step closer. "I'm not."

Keegan sighs, turning toward the unlit fireplace. With a blink of his eyes, flames shoot over the hearth. "Don't make me regret this."

"We won't." Murphy and I say in unison.

Keegan moves toward the door. "I'll meet you in the courtyard at noon." He pauses. "We'll need to leave the castle grounds. I don't want anyone else finding out."

"Agreed," Murphy answers.

"No." Keegan looks up. "Just Adria... alone." He leaves the room, closing the doors behind him.

"No bloody way am I letting him take you off castle grounds without me." Murphy barely waited for the doors to close before objecting. "That's just asking for danger."

Holding my hands up in surrender mode. "Murphy, don't make a big deal out of this."

"A big deal? That's what you think this will be? A big deal?" Anger pours off him. "You barely know this guy for two days, yet you trust him enough to leave the safety of the compound, alone?"

"Murphy, please try to understand. It's my life I'm putting in danger, not yours." I send warm waves of soft energy through our connection. "Nothing's going to happen. He's not going to hurt me."

"How do you know, Adria?" He sits, putting his head in his hands. "We barely know Keegan. What if he's working with Astrid? What if he's part of her plan." His voice becomes weaker.

"He's not working with anyone. Yes, he has secrets, but you have to trust me when I say, he won't hurt me." I sit beside him.

"Gods, Adria. Do you know what you're asking?" His words are barely louder than a whisper.

I lace my fingers through his. "I do, and if the table was turned, I would be giving you shit about doing the same." He rests his head on my shoulder. "I can take care of myself."

"I know you can. I just don't want you to be put in a situation where you have to."

"I'm a First Elemental. You can't protect me from everything."

"I can sure as hell try." He kisses me on the forehead.

"He's not going to hurt me. Astrid is stronger than Llyr or Shu think. I don't have time to hang around here, signing paperwork and settling disputes between lessers. Keegan is the answer."

Murphy looks down in defeat. "If you get an inkling of anything out of the ordinary, don't hesitate." I know what he's saying and nod in agreement.

An hour later, I'm wearing running gear and waiting in the courtyard with Murphy. Keegan exits the castle carrying two backpacks and wearing a neon pink and green wind suit. "Remind me to let him use my computer and Amazon account later," I whisper, making Murphy laugh for the first time in a few hours.

"I took the liberty of bringing some items we might need." Keegan hands me one of the packs. "There are snacks and water inside." He slides his pack on his back. "Ready?"

I copy his motions, "Ready." Murphy turns to Keegan.

"Take care of her." Keegan nods in agreement, and I follow him through the front gate.

CHAPTER 5

*K*eegan leads me through the village and several miles past without speaking. The silence is uncomfortable, and I'm questioning my choice of trainer. We stop in front of a burned-out cottage, miles from anywhere.

"What's this place?" I stare at the remains of what was once a flower garden.

"My home." He shifts from foot to foot. "It burned down when I was a kid. *I* burned it down when I was a kid." I wait for him to continue. "I was a toddler when I set my first fire. I had no clue what I was doing or that the fire was even coming from me." He pauses for a second time. "My mother would find them throughout the cottage, nothing she couldn't put out quickly, until one day... she couldn't."

"You started a fire she couldn't put out." I fill in the blanks.

He sniffs loudly. "She tried. I remember the fire

growing larger and her struggling against the flames." Tears slide down his cheek. "I killed her. I killed my mother." I fight the urge to reach out to him. "After she died, I lived with my grandmother for a while. She blamed me for her death and wasn't... kind." He pauses. "She was right to blame me. It was my fault."

I touch his shoulder, hoping to offer comfort. "You were a child with no clue what you were doing. You can't blame yourself for something like that."

Wiping his face with the back of his hand. "That's where you're wrong. There's no one to blame *but* me. If I hadn't started the fire, she'd be alive today." I don't know what to say. There are no right words for something like this. He wipes his face again. "Do you see why I don't want anything to do with this power? It only brings heartache."

"Keegan, you started a fire in a controlled area yesterday with the blink of an eye. You were in complete control. You have more skill than many lessers I've met. The power we hold in our blood isn't a curse. It's a blessing." Llyr would be proud of my words.

"How can you say that, Adria? I killed my own mother and was hated because of it." He sits on a large boulder at the edge of the path.

"I didn't discover my element until last year, but I understand what it is to grow up being hated. My mother died when I was a toddler, and I was raised in the foster care system. It wasn't the best of times. I know what it's like to carry pain around, buried deep inside. Since then, I've come to realize my element isn't a curse, it's a blessing.

We have the best of both worlds, human and elemental." I move toward the boulder.

"You'll forgive me if I don't agree," he retorts.

"I don't need you to agree. I need you to teach me." For the first time since leaving the castle grounds this afternoon, Keegan makes eye contact with me.

"Okay." He stands.

"Here?" I ask, looking around the remains.

"This is the place I discovered my ability. Maybe it'll be that for you too." His voice is full of emotion. "Follow me."

I follow him around the ruins to what used to be the backyard. An old swing shifts in the breeze, evidence of the young family that once lived here. The remnants of a rotted-out storage building sit at an angle with barely enough walls to keep it from collapsing on itself. The doors and windows are wide open, allowing the elements to wreak havoc on the ruined contents inside. This reminds me of a scene straight from a horror movie. "Keegan, are you sure this is the best place? I'm not liking the vibes around here."

He stops walking. "I do. We're miles away from another human. No one comes out here anymore. This is the perfect place." He sets his backpack down next to the dilapidated shed. I copy his motions and follow him to the center of the yard. He sighs. "It took me years to discover that I control fire through my eyes. Before then, I had no clue how I started them."

His words snag a memory from the fight with Brigit. I remember Llyr covering Astrid's eyes and telling me to take out Brigit's. I nod in agreement.

"When I want something to burn, I simply think of the action in my mind, picture the fire and look at the item."

"Sounds simple enough," I answer. "Is that what I need to do?"

He sighs. "I've spent years running from fire, trying to figure out how to teach it to someone else is not something I thought I'd ever be doing."

"I understand." Keegan turns toward the edge of the overgrown property.

"See that bush?" He points.

"Yes."

"I want you to look at it, really look at it. As you do, I want you to form a picture in your mind of fire. Not a huge fire, but a small, easily controlled one."

I follow his instructions, picturing a campfire-size fire. Nothing happens. "Are you doing it?" he asks.

"Yes," I whisper. I repeat the steps, and this time a small puff of smoke rises from the bush.

"That's it," he says, showing a small amount of enthusiasm for the first time since we left. "Keep going." I picture a raging fire this time, hoping it will grow larger. Instead of smoke, small flames leap from the top.

"Was that me?" I ask in shock.

"Yes." He smiles. "Again," he commands. Small flames turn into a raging fire within seconds as the bush is completely engulfed.

"Okay, that's enough." His voice sounds distressed. I send a wall of water straight into the flames, extinguishing them on contact.

"That comes in handy." He turns to me. "Good job. What did you do that made the difference?"

"Honestly, I don't know. I pictured a large fire and suddenly that happened." I find a bush several feet away from the first. Focusing my energy, I envision the bush turning into flames. Slowly, the bush follows my command, and flames shoot from the top.

"You've got a great start. We'll work more tomorrow." He looks down. "I'm sorry to be so intense earlier." He runs a hand through his ebony hair, mimicking a movement I've seen Murphy do many times. "Being able to control fire has never brought me anything but pain."

"It's time to embrace your gift, Keegan." I turn toward the ruins of the house. "Burn it down." He looks up in question. I nod toward the house. "The best way to clear away the things that haunt us is by confronting them head-on. Burn it down."

He turns to the ruins. "I don't think I can. It's the only thing I have left of her."

"Does being here bring you joy or pain?"

"Pain," he whispers, staring at the remains of his childhood. Within seconds, flames completely engulf the structure. We watch in silence until nothing but warm, red embers remain, and the sun is low in the sky.

"Leave the sadness and everything negative this house represented to you, here. What remains is nothing more than memories lost to the flames." He nods, taking two water bottles from his backpack and handing me one.

"Thank you." His voice sounds lighter, less burdened than before.

"We need to get back." I drink half the water in one gulp.

Keegan stands, offering me a hand. I ignore it. "Yes, we do. Murphy will have my head on a stick if we're out here much longer."

We jog through the village on our way back to the castle. Keegan still isn't speaking much, but his energy is lighter than earlier. The village feels different than I remember from yesterday. The welcoming feeling is gone, replaced by something that feels much darker. The setting sun casts an eerie glow over the buildings, forming wide shadows along the ground. The hairs on my arm stand on end and my skin feels electrified. Something's wrong. "Keegan, do you feel that?" He stops near the village fountain. "I don't know how to describe it, but something's different."

We walk toward the soda fountain. The lights are off and the doors are locked. "Brenna's most likely in bed." He turns back to the center. "Maybe we're just being paranoid. Living in California can do that to a person."

"Agreed, but I've never been one for paranoia." I scan the horizon for anything out of the ordinary, seeing nothing. For the first time since becoming a First Elemental, I call on my energy to feel for danger. Pulling from my core, my throat, and my eyes, I picture the elements combining, joining together into a large ball of energy. Instinctively, I push the ball to every corner of the island, and in an instant, it's returned. Pictures instantly form in my mind. An image of a castle pops into view. Not Brigit's castle, but a smaller one, hanging on the side of a cliff. A beautiful red-headed woman is standing on the pinnacle with her arms outstretched. Below her, a hoard of lessers is roaring in delight. As soon as the image leaves, the world goes black.

......

My eyes open to familiar red walls and horrible decor. "Murphy?" I whisper in confusion.

"Aye." A warm hand caresses my cheek. "I'm here."

I struggle to sit up. "What happened? How did I get back here?"

Murphy sits on the edge of the bed, pulling the edge down with his weight. "Keegan carried you."

"All the way from the village?"

"Aye."

"Is he okay?" Looking around the room, it's just the two of us.

"He's fine. He's resting. What happened out there?" he asks, continuing to caress my cheek.

"I don't know. I think maybe I had a vision." Memories flood my mind and I jump out of bed and head straight to the window. "Oh, my gods. I saw her, I saw Astrid. She's here."

Murphy moves to my side. "What are you talking about? Keegan didn't say anything about seeing Astrid."

"That's because he didn't see her. It was a vision." I rub my head trying to figure out how to explain something I don't understand. "When we got to the village, the energy was... off. The air had an electrical feel to it. I sensed something was different." I rub my hands across the goosebumps forming. "I combined the energy of water, air, and fire and sent it out in search of an explanation." I turn toward Murphy. "That's when I saw her, and she wasn't alone."

"Who was with her?"

"An army," I whisper. "She had a freaking army."

"Where?" He paces the floor in front of me.

"I don't know, but they were here, in Iceland. I'm sure of it." I grab a piece of paper and begin sketching the castle from my vision.

"This is where she is." I hand the paper to Murphy.

"Is this a castle?"

"I think so. It was much smaller than this one, but a castle nonetheless."

"What does this mean?" He moves toward the phone.

"It means we don't have to worry about *when* she'll get here. She's already here."

"Rhys?" Murphy says, holding the ancient phone receiver to his face. "Could you and Keegan come to Adria's room, immediately?" He hangs up, moving to my side. "Maybe one of them will recognize your drawing."

"Come in," I call to the door a minute later. Keegan walks in, followed by Rhys.

"It's good to see you moving around." Keegan's changed out of his retro jogging suit, into a pair of jeans and long sleeve knit shirt, reminding me of the typical California male.

"Agreed, thanks for getting me back here. That was a long way for you to carry me."

"What exactly happened? One minute you were standing there, the next you were on the ground. I couldn't get you to wake up." Keegan steps closer.

I sit on the couch, sinking into the plush cushions. "I had a vision. I'm guessing that's what it was. Hell, I don't know anymore." Murphy hands me the drawing. "Do either of you recognize this?" Keegan takes the picture.

"What is it?" he asks, studying the picture.

"It's what I saw."

Keegan shakes his head. "Doesn't look familiar to me." He hands it to Rhys who studies the picture intently.

"It could possibly be Castle Grimsgil." He moves the picture closer to his eyes. "If it is, it's changed since I was there last. I remember it being nothing more than ruins. But this," he points to the hastily drawn turret, "is identical to Grimsgil and the only one of its kind in Iceland."

Murphy moves toward Rhys. "Are you sure?"

"No. But that's the only castle I know of with turrets like that."

"Where's this castle?" Murphy's energy is heavy.

"North, almost as far as you can go. It sits on top of a glacier, high in the black mountains, and is surrounded by nothing but ice and snow." Murphy and I exchange looks.

"Thank you, Rhys. You may go. Keegan, please stay." Murphy dismisses the older lesser.

"What the hell's going on?" Keegan asks after Rhys closes the door behind him.

Murphy looks at me with raised eyebrows. I know he's asking how much we need to divulge. I sigh. "It's a long story."

Keegan sits in a chair that looks like it belongs in a dungeon rather than a bedroom and crosses his legs. "I have all the time in the world."

"You know the particulars of me and my story. You

know that in order to gain the power of fire I had to kill Brigit." He nods. "Only a child of a First can kill a First."

"Your father is Llyr, making you the child of a First."

"He is, but there's something else I've kept secret." Keegan looks confused. "Llyr isn't my only connection to elemental power. Shu, the god of air is my grandfather."

"Your father is the god of water, and your *grandfather* is the god of air? Holy shit. That's how you were able to get us to the beach. We really did fly."

"And when I killed Brigit, I became the goddess of fire."

Keegan laughs. "Then what the hell are you scared about? You hold the power of three elements. No one in their right mind would dare to threaten you."

Murphy laughs at the irony. "You've got that right."

"What am I not understanding?" Keegan asks.

"Only the child of a First can kill a First."

Keegan nods in agreement. "That's why you were able to kill Brigit."

"Yes, but that means a child of a First can kill me." He wrinkles his forehead.

"I'm not good at riddles." He looks between the two of us. "Do you think I'm the child of a First?"

"No, but there is one out there, and she's closer than we thought." I stand from the couch and walk to the window. "Brigit had a son and a daughter. When I killed Brigit, I also killed her son, Earwyn." Keegan sits quietly, waiting for me to continue. "Her daughter, Astrid was there also."

"Astrid was her daughter?" he asks. "I knew her when I was a teenager. She and an older kid would get milkshakes from the diner." He pauses. "She was Brigit's daughter?"

"Aye, and I'm guessing the older kid was Earwyn. Since their deaths, she's pissed."

"From what I remember, she stayed that way," Keegan adds. "You think Astrid is back and coming to kill you?"

"We don't think, we know," Murphy answers.

"What makes you so sure? She was just an angry kid." Something about his posture seems different. He's subconsciously bouncing his leg, clearly holding more information than he's willing to share.

"She killed Dagda," Murphy blurts.

Keegan scoots forward in his seat. "Dagda, the god of earth?"

"The very same," I answer sarcastically.

"Well, shit. What does that mean exactly? I mean, I know he's dead, but does she become the new goddess of earth like you did fire?"

"That's exactly what it means."

He stands, pacing behind the chair. "Let me see if I have this right." He scratches his head. "Astrid, the daughter of Brigit and the only one capable of killing a First, has killed the god of earth and assumed the position for herself, and now she's coming here to kill you?"

"Yep, that's it in a nutshell," Murphy answers for me.

"And you two think she's at this Castle Grimsgil, the highest damn point in Iceland?"

"I'm sure of it," I answer. "During my vision, I saw Astrid in this very castle." I shake the paper at him. "She wasn't alone. There was an army of lessers with her, all under her command."

Keegan sits back in the chair. "We're sitting ducks. Is there anyone here that would be loyal to her?"

I shrug. "I don't know, but you remember the fire after our run. That wasn't an accident. It was a warning."

"Or it was a test of our defenses. Whoever started the fire got into the compound easily," Murphy adds.

"That's my job to fix," Keegan announces.

"Aye, 'tis."

"Then what?" Keegan asks. "Do we sit here and wait for her to attack, or do we beat her to the punch?"

"What do you have in mind?" I ask.

He stands again. "You have an army of water, air, and fire lessers ready to fight for you. Astrid has earth and a few rogue fire lessers. Why not beat her at her own game, and attack the castle before she attacks you?"

I look to Murphy. "I have a problem with sending people to their death."

"That's what lessers were made to do," Keegan retorts.

Murphy sighs. "He's right. I know you don't want anyone to die, but attacking her on her own ground will be the last thing she expects."

"It'll also mean less loss of life for us," Keegan adds.

"How many fire lessers live here on the grounds or near?" I ask whoever has the answer.

"Seventy-five, plus or minus a few," Keegan answers quickly. "I did my homework."

"Have you all thought about the fact that the lessers who are with Astrid are most likely the new ones, the monstrosities Brigit created? They won't be like the ones here. They're faster, stronger, and insane." Memories of the one at the California compound come to mind.

Keegan genuinely looks confused. "New kinds of lessers?"

"Aye. They've been around for centuries but kept hidden for most of it."

"Their favorite meal is human flesh," I blurt.

Keegan looks stunned. "Are you pulling my leg?"

"Why would I pull your leg?" Murphy looks confused, making me laugh.

"It's American slang. He's asking if we're playing a trick on him."

"Ah. No, we're not pulling anyone's leg." He winks at me, proud of his slang usage.

I stand from the couch. "Let's get some sleep. We have a few hours until everyone else wakes up. We'll meet tomorrow to decide our options."

"Aye," Murphy agrees. Keegan stands, shaking Murphy's hand, before leaving the room. I crawl into bed, flipping the covers open for Murphy before the door completely closes.

"I'm too exhausted to think." I pat the empty spot next to me. "Come on big guy, let's get some shut-eye."

"Big guy?" He laughs, strips down to his boxers, and crawls next to me. The heat radiating from him warms my tired muscles, and I assume the position of the little spoon.

"Are you sure you're okay?" he whispers into my neck.

"Yes, I promise." Lacing my fingers through his, I pull his hand to my stomach. "Right now, I just want to sleep next to my favorite person in the world."

"I love you," he whispers.

"I love you, too."

CHAPTER 6

*T*he sun is high in the sky when my eyes crack open. I'm still wrapped in a Murphy cocoon, and my back begs to be shifted to a new position. I wiggle free of his hold, heading to the bathroom. "Where are you going?" his sleepy voice whispers.

"It's late. I'm surprised Rhys hasn't knocked on the door already."

He takes a deep breath, rolling over. "Me, too. What time is it?"

One quick look at the ancient gold leaf clock, courtesy of Brigit, tells me it's almost noon. "Oh, my gods. You don't want to know."

"That late, huh?" He pats the bed next to him. "Why don't you come back to bed, and we'll stay here all day?" His voice is deep, sexy, and tempting.

"Do you think we're ready for that?" He knows what I'm asking. Murphy takes my hand into his, seductively kissing each knuckle. His lips elicit chill bumps to every surface of my body. "This isn't an answer." He continues his kissing assault, moving to my wrist.

"If we wait for the perfect time, there won't ever be one." He moves up my arm. "I love you, Adria." He pulls away, making eye contact with me. "This may sound cliché, but I don't want to be with anyone but you, ever. You're the first thing I think about when I wake up and the last thing I think about before going to sleep." He pulls me into his lap, my legs straddling his hips. "I knew I loved you from the moment you put that blade in my spine at the compound." I laugh at the memory.

"You never did learn lesson one," I remind him. His arms are my home. "You're the best version of everything I am."

He kisses me deeply. "You make me that way. I'm a better version of me when I'm with you." He's right, there will never be a perfect time. Especially now that Astrid's in Iceland. I slowly rotate my hips, eliciting a moan. I repeat the motion, receiving the same results. "Gods, Adria. You might want to stop."

I pull away enough to see his face. "What if I don't want to stop?" His eyes dilate in an instant, and he flips our position, putting me on the bottom and him on top. His arousal is evident, and I long to wrap every part of me around it. Murphy pulls off the thin tank top I'm wearing, revealing my breasts.

"Gods, you're beautiful." He lowers himself on top of me.

"So are you." His sleep pants are hanging low on his hips, and I long to pull them the rest of the way down.

Every place our skin meets is on fire. A loud knock on the door makes both of us freeze. "Shit."

"Ignore it." He continues kissing my neck. The knock sounds again, louder. "Go away!" he shouts, making me snicker a laugh.

"I could do that, but we need to talk," Keegan calls through the locked door. "I feel really awkward right now," he adds.

Murphy sits up, running his hands through frizzy curls. "Can it wait?"

"Um, it could, but it's past noon, and it's important enough for me to interrupt whatever I'm interrupting." He laughs awkwardly. "It has to do with the fire in the courtyard."

"Dammit. I'm sorry, Adria." He stands, pulling his pants back in place and sliding on a t-shirt. "Give me a minute." He calls to the door.

"Okay, is Adria in there? I mean, it is her room and all, so that means she's probably in there... gods, this is getting worse by the minute." His words make me laugh. "Sorry, I'm not good at this sort of thing."

"I'm here Keegan. Give us a minute?" I ask toward the door.

"I'll wait in your office." He pauses. "Okay, bye."

I can't hold the laugh back. "Why do I feel sorry for him?" Murphy joins my laugh.

"He wasn't at his best," he agrees, pulling me from the bed. "To be continued." Soft, gentle kisses leave want in their wake.

"Ten minutes?" He nods, leaving my room for his. I

take a quick shower, pull my hair into a makeshift bun and slide on a pair of leggings and a sweatshirt.

Eleven minutes later, we enter the office to find Keegan staring out of the corner window. He turns quickly. "I'm sorry about earlier." He steps closer.

"Don't give it another thought. What news do you have?" I sit behind the large, ornate, hideously ugly desk.

Keegan sighs, walking to the chair in front. "After our talk last night, I couldn't stop thinking about the monstrous lessers you mentioned. I did a little research and was able to find these." He pulls a stack of papers out of a makeshift folder in his hands. "It got me thinking about something from my childhood." He rambles through the papers, pulling out what looks like an old newspaper clipping, and slides them toward me. "I found some interesting articles from local papers."

-*Rash of Mysterious Deaths Blamed on Mountain Wolves*-, I read the headline out loud. Murphy wrinkles his forehead, taking the paper from me. "Keegan, what does this have to do with the fire in the courtyard?"

Keegan hands me another article. This headline reads - *Fires Blamed on Lightening*-. "I'm not following you. Tell me what you're thinking."

He sighs. "I think these monster lessers have been in Iceland for a very long time. I found articles dating back over a hundred years, all with similar headlines." I'm becoming impatient waiting for him to explain how this is related to the fire. He sighs. "Not only have they been on the island a long time, but I think Brigit created them on the mountain where Astrid is now."

"Keegan, what exactly are you saying?" Murphy's as impatient as me.

"I'm saying you're right. Astrid does have an army." He looks down at his stack of papers. "An army of over one thousand monstrous lessers, ready to fight for their queen."

"What the bloody hell?" Murphy walks toward Keegan. "One thousand? Are you sure?"

Keegan shakes his head. "No. But after researching all night, it makes sense."

I stand, moving toward my new security chief. "Please help me understand all of his. You're talking in circles. Why would you think that Brigit housed over a thousand monsters at that castle?"

He sighs, clearly uncomfortable. "Because I've been there."

Murphy steps in front of me protectively. "Why didn't you tell us this last night?" I step around my gigantic bodyguard.

"It didn't seem relevant," he answers.

Murphy moves forward. "It didn't seem relevant?" His words are calculated and precise. "You were in the damn room while Adria drew a picture of a castle that you have actually been to. How the hell is it not relevant?"

"Let me explain." Keegan backs away.

"Please do," Murphy warns.

"After my mother died, I didn't know where I belonged. My grandmother blamed me for her death and wanted nothing to do with me. The only reason she agreed to let me live there was for the government assistance she received for my care." He sighs, and his story strikes a familiar chord. "I ran away too many times to count. My grandmother didn't care, she was still getting her money. Brigit found me." His words are soft. "I wasn't any older than seven or eight. I'd been living in the village and the burned-out cottage, hiding in sheds, sleeping under porches, stealing food and clothes when I could." He pauses in thought. "I remember the first time I saw her. She was shopping in the village with a boy about my age and a younger girl."

"Earwyn and Astrid," Murphy says to me.

"She was the most beautiful woman I'd ever seen. Her hair looked like fire, and her face was that of an angel." I fight the urge to cringe. "I watched the three of them go in and out of stores, watched how she made sure they were safe and protected, and I followed them home."

"You followed them here? To the castle?"

He nods. "I hid in the outlying storage buildings for a few weeks, stealing food from the garden or trash, until one day Aiden found me."

I'd almost forgotten Earwyn's birth name was Aiden. Brigit changed it to a water name, all part of her plan to overtake Llyr and the element of water.

"He tied me up and went to find Brigit."

"Yep, that's Earwyn. He was lovely." Murphy's words are full of sarcasm.

"What happened?" I ask.

"She was kind to me. After she realized I was a hybrid and a runaway, she let me live here, at the castle." He turns to face us.

"What the bloody hell?" Murphy's words are laced with venom. "I brought you in to be our chief of security, and you tell me you lived with the damn goddess of fire, the very one who tried to kill both of us. That she was your surrogate mother? Astrid, the one who is determined to kill Adria, and you are some sort of adopted siblings. Are you fucking kidding me? Is this some kind of joke to you?" I've never seen Murphy this angry. I put my hand on his shoulder sending calming energy through our touch. He pulls away, moving closer to Keegan.

Keegan raises his hands in front of his chest in a defensive move. "Murphy, let me continue. I know what this sounds like."

"Do you, Keegan? Because this sounds like a bunch of shit to me."

"Let him continue," I echo, keeping my voice level and calm. Murphy closes his eyes in response, working to keep his emotions at bay. "Go on," I encourage Keegan.

He lowers his hands. "It didn't take me long to realize who she pretended to be and who she was, were two different people. Aiden and Astrid weren't allowed to play. Neither were allowed toys other than small items they could practice burning. They were expected to be perfect, in every way." He lowers his head. "Aiden made her angry often and spent weeks locked in his room or the dungeon below."

"It's no surprise Brigit wasn't the mother of the year," Murphy adds.

"After one particularly crazy outburst, she sent Aiden to America to train with the elementals there. She said it was better to be away from all the luxuries of the castle."

"How were you at Castle Grimsgil?" I interrupt wherever his story is leading.

He rubs his charcoal-colored hair. "A few weeks after she sent Aiden away, she took me and Astrid there, to Grimsgil. I remember it being a really long drive and colder than any place I'd ever been."

"What did you see?" Murphy asks.

"Lessers who looked normal, only they weren't." He pauses in thought. "On more than one occasion, I witnessed groups of people being brought into the castle but never leaving." He pauses, deep in thought. "Growing up in the human world, I'd never seen fire elementals so comfortable with their element. They would burn anything in their line of sight just for shits and giggles." He sniffs. "I didn't know what was going on, but I knew it was wrong. I ran away and never looked back."

"Keegan, do we look dumb?" Murphy asks.

Keegan wrinkles his forehead. "No?"

"Murphy," I whisper. I don't blame him for being angry, but my first instinct told me Keegan was trustworthy, and I still believe he is. "What happened when you ran away?"

"Brenna found me."

"She saved you?"

He nods, wiping a tear from his cheek. "I'm sorry. I should've told you last night. I understand if you want to put me in the dungeon."

"The dungeon?"

"Aye," Murphy answers. "Llyr isn't the only one with a prison beneath their castle.

"Keegan, when you were at Castle Grimsgil, you saw thousands of these monster lessers?"

"I never saw them all in one place, but there was a

revolving door of visitors. All of them participated in the 'games' she held." He holds up air quotes.

"Were they all monsters?" Murphy asks.

Keegan shrugs. "I don't know. It seemed that way to a child." He moves closer, handing me a sheet of paper with an old black-and-white photo. "There's one more thing."

I study the picture. A man in his early twenties stands in front of a burned body. Blood drips from his chin and he's holding what looks like the remains of a human arm in his hand. "Why are you showing me this?"

"Look at the eyes," he urges.

I study the eyes of the man in the picture. The face staring back at me looks vaguely familiar. "Am I supposed to know who this is?"

The double doors to the office swing open as Rhys enters. "Lunch is served, Adria." He announces with an awkward smile. No doubt he's proud that he used my name without being reminded. I face him with the picture in my hand.

"Thank you, Rhys. We'll be there shortly." I glance at the photo and make the connection Keegan hoped I would. Rhys shuts the doors, leaving the three of us alone.

Holy shit. The man in the photo and the man who made our lunch are one and the same. Rhys is a monster lesser. I stand in silence, not sure how to process the connection I just made. "What is it?" Murphy asks, coming to my side. I hand him the picture and watch as he wrinkles his forehead in confusion. "What am I missing?"

"That is a picture of Rhys when he was at Grimsgil." Keegan steps closer. "Something about him seemed familiar the first night I was here but I didn't connect all the pieces until I found that picture." He takes it from Murphy.

"You think the man in the picture is Rhys? The same Rhys who just came in here after making lunch for us all. That Rhys?" Murphy's face is a mixture of confusion and repulsion.

"I'm certain of it," Keegan answers. "Plus, it has his name on the back, so there's that." He points to a smeared, poorly written name on the back of the picture.

"You think he set the fire in the courtyard?" I cross my arms over my chest. Rhys has been with me since day one. Truth is, I've gotten attached to him.

"Could be, I don't know," Keegan answers. "There could be more than just him living here." His words unlock a new fear. I hadn't even thought about that possibility. I assumed the fire elementals at the castle were lessers in full support of the goddess, whether that goddess was Brigit or me.

"It would make sense that there's more." Murphy takes the words out of my mouth. He turns to me. "Has Rhys ever given you a reason to doubt his loyalty?"

I shake my head. "No. He's only ever been kind, helpful, and on top of his responsibilities."

"Why don't we just ask him?"

Murphy and I both look at Keegan. "Sure, we'll just invite him to lunch." My words are meant to be sarcastic, but Keegan agrees readily.

"That's actually not a bad idea," Murphy agrees. "Invite him to eat with us."

"He's not going to eat human food. Lessers don't eat," I retort.

"No, but he might relish an opportunity to sit with the goddess of fire, at her table."

"Especially if he did start the courtyard fire," Keegan adds to Murphy's words.

Several minutes pass before the three of us are sitting at the ornate dining table. Rhys has a simple bowl of rice, grilled chicken, and a mixture of fruits and vegetables. Even with my lack of appetite, it looks delicious. Rhys brings in a container of dressings, setting it between us. "Rhys?"

He stops. "Yes, ma'am?"

"Would you care to join us?" I ask, slowly mixing my concoction together. Rhys stares at me dumbfounded.

"Ma'am?"

"Would you care to join us? I'm not very hungry, and I hate for this delicious lunch to go to waste." I scoot my bowl toward an empty seat.

Rhys has turned pale. "I... Thank you, but I have a bowl set for myself in the kitchen. I wouldn't want to impose on you, your high... Adria."

"Don't be silly. You don't have to eat alone. Sit out here, with us." I smile warmly. "I insist."

It's clear he doesn't know what to say. "If you insist. Let me get my bowl. I wouldn't dream of taking yours." He turns, leaving the dining room. Murphy raises an eyebrow in my direction, and I shrug in response. Rhys returns moments later carrying a bowl identical to ours and a glass of water. "Thank you. I've never been invited to eat at this table before. To be honest, I'm a little out of my league." He laughs a short, awkward laugh while sitting across from me.

"See, that's a shame. You spend your time making sure all of my needs are met, yet we've never really gotten to know each other." I continue moving food around in the bowl.

"It's my job to serve you, your hi... Adria," he answers nervously.

"How long have you served the goddess of fire?" Keegan asks, taking the pressure off me.

"Twelve years," Rhys answers. "It's been a pleasure." He looks at me. "Oh, I don't mean that you and Brigit are the same, just that it's been a pleasure to serve in my capacity."

I wave my hand. "I understand what you mean. I should've asked you to join us months ago. I apologize for that. I don't want you to feel like a servant, just an employee. I'm afraid I haven't done much to change that."

Rhys smiles, taking a bite of his rice bowl. Murphy raises his eyebrows watching Rhys eat human food.

"Have you lived here, at the castle the entire time?" This time it's Murphy asking.

Rhys relaxes in his seat slightly. He's feeling more comfortable. "Yes. I started working for Brigit when my father retired."

"Your father?" I ask. "Did he work for Brigit too?"

"He did. I took over his job when he left. Just as he did when his father left." He takes another bite of his lunch. "I guess you could say it's a family tradition."

"I bet," Keegan answers. "Did your father live here while he worked for Brigit?"

"Yes," Rhys answers. "Why do you ask?"

I take a small bite of pineapple and chicken. "Just getting to know you." I smile.

Murphy pulls the photo from his back pocket. "Keegan found this picture earlier. It has your name on the back." He hands it to Rhys. "Do you know anything about it?"

Rhys takes the photo. "Huh. That's my name alright, but I don't remember taking this picture." He laughs. "What's that on my face?" Rhys's body language has returned to rigid.

Keegan stands, moving closer to Rhys. "Blood," he answers.

Rhys returns the photo to the table and stands. "Thank you for the invitation, Adria. It's a memory I'll cherish for a while." He methodically pushes his chair under the table and moves back toward the kitchen.

"I think you might want to stay." Keegan moves behind Rhys, who freezes in place. Murphy moves to Keegan's side. Both men are ready for whatever's about to happen. Rhys turns toward them. His eyes have turned from their normal copper hue to bright red.

"It's true. That's me, but I'm not that man anymore." He extends his hands in front of his body and crosses them at the wrist. "Put me in the prison below. I have no way to prove my innocence other than to allow you to do with me what you want." Keegan pulls a pair of handcuffs out of his back pocket and begins to wrap them around my butler's wrists. Rhys looks at me. "Adria, I want nothing but the best for our element and for you. Brigit was a cruel, horrible monster who created creatures in her image. She killed innocents and forced us to do the same. I rebelled years ago and refused to follow her ways. I owe you my life and my complete loyalty. You did what I couldn't. You killed that bitch."

"Wait," I call after Keegan who has blindfolded Rhys and leading him out of the room. He turns him toward me. "Did you start the fire in the courtyard?"

Rhys sighs deeply. "No, your highness, I did not."

"Do you know who did?"

He pauses before answering. "I'm sorry to say, I don't. I would've disposed of them if I had." I nod, watching Keegan lead him out of the room to the depths of the castle.

CHAPTER 7

urphy and I stand face to face in the gym of the castle. After lunch and sending Rhys to the bowels of who knows where, I need to sweat off my feelings. "Again," I say, breathing hard. Murphy sighs and returns to his side of the sparring mat.

"Working both of us into exhaustion isn't going to solve anything." He lands a punch in my shoulder.

"That was weak. Hit me like you would any other training partner or elemental." I ignore his moment of clarity. "You wouldn't hit Earwyn like that."

"Adria, this isn't the answer."

"Dammit, I know. But I don't know what else to do right now." I sit down in defeat on a large yoga ball. "I hate this!"

He sits on the floor in front of me. "You're not going to have the answers to every problem in the world."

"No, but I'm expected to have an answer for this one."

I stand, kicking the ball across the room, and hitting the entrance door. The glass inside explodes on impact.

"Okay, David Beckham, I'm putting you in a time-out." He steers me toward a bench that's too heavy to kick.

"I'm sorry. I don't mean to take it out on you." I take a deep breath. "Knowing that Astrid's in Iceland with a hoard of monster elementals is bad enough, but to know one of them was in this household, in my room... I trusted him, Murphy." My head lowers to my hands. "If he didn't start the fire, then who did? Are there more of those monsters here?" Maybe Rhys was telling the truth. Maybe he has changed. "Is it possible for one of the monster lessers to become a regular elemental?"

Murphy sits beside me. "I don't know. We didn't have proof they existed until you. They're undiscovered territory. No one knows anything about them."

"Except for Astrid," I whisper.

"Aye, except Astrid," he echoes. Murphy slides his fingers through mine.

"Seems like we're left without a choice." Murphy looks up in question. "She has spies here at the castle, that's obvious from Rhys and the fire. She's building an army, from which we won't survive. We have to attack her before she attacks us. We have to take her by surprise." I lay my head on the wall behind me. "Gods, I hate having to make decisions like this. Decisions that will send people to their deaths." A tear streams down my cheek.

Murphy pulls me into his lap. "I know you do. But you're making the right choice. We're sitting ducks here. Attacking first will give us the advantage of surprise."

I nod, sniffing loudly. Murphy's the only one I allow myself to be vulnerable with. I don't let anyone else see my weaknesses. Knowing he's with me no matter the outcome is the true meaning of love. "Thank you." I wrap my arms around him, pulling him tight. "I love you."

"I know," he answers with a smirk, lightening the mood. "I'll call Llyr and Shu. We can't do this alone. To defeat her and the hoard, we'll need water and air and anything else we can find."

The thought of seeing my father and grandfather again lifts my spirits. "Shu will be happy some of the items have started arriving for the remodel." The reality of our immediate future hits me like a bomb. "I'm going to have to master all three elements, aren't I?"

"Aye."

"How long do you think we have?"

"I don't know. I'll ask Shu to send spies. We need eyes on them constantly. I want to know when Astrid eats, sleeps, and shits. The more information we gather, the stronger our chances will be."

"Our plans need to remain a secret." I look at our joined hands. "I don't want news getting back to Astrid."

"How are we going to explain an army of water and air elementals arriving and training, without locking up every fire elemental in the dungeon?" Murphy has a good point.

"We'll figure that out later," I answer.

"Aye." He stands, pulling me with him. "I'll call them now." He leans down, kissing me on the forehead. "You're the strongest being on this planet. Remember that. You are the secret weapon."

I huff a laugh. "A secret weapon who can't control her powers. Astrid has an army at her side."

"So do you."

"I wish I were as confident as you."

......

I haven't seen Murphy since the gym, and I'm okay with being alone. My room, Brigit's room, is dark and provides a good hiding spot to sit and sulk. I never wanted to be the person that makes the choice to send people to their possible deaths, but here we are, and it pisses me off. Truthfully, the only way to defeat her is with elements. At best, I'm at the kindergarten level when it comes to control. A soft knock on the door draws me from my stupor.

"Yes?" I ask.

"It's me, it's Keegan." He pauses. "Can I come in?"

"Yes."

He opens the door, moving to the chair across from the couch I'm sprawled across. "Murphy filled me in on your plans. He also told me to keep it on the down low."

"How's Rhys?" I ask, ignoring his words.

Keegan looks down. "I made sure he was comfortable. He's upset, but his behavior seems strange to me."

I look up. "How?"

"He doesn't act guilty." He grunts, lost for words. "He doesn't have the body language of someone hiding their guilt. He's been nothing but cooperative. He's answered every question and adamantly denies any connection to Astrid or other monster lessers."

"What does that mean?" I sit up.

"It could mean he's had many years to perfect his skills, or he could be telling the truth." Nothing would make me happier than to know Rhys wasn't spying on me for the past few months.

"I'll go visit him tomorrow. Maybe he'll be honest with me, or I'll be able to see through his farce." I scratch my head, making my hair a bundle of tangles. "Keegan, I need you to train me."

He looks down with a shrug. "I don't know what else I can teach you. You started the fires with your eyes. There's really nothing more I can teach."

I stand, moving toward him. "Dammit, Keegan. I need to master this element, and you're the only one around here I trust."

"I appreciate that, but someone with more control would be better. I'm just a hybrid with a mild amount of control. You need someone who has mastered the element."

"There's no one! Besides you, I don't know who I can or can't trust." Frustration turns into anger and threatens to burst through my skin.

"The person with the most power doesn't live at the castle and isn't someone you would run into normally." He stumbles over his words.

"Someone in Iceland or even in the village?"

He shifts from foot to foot. "Brenna," he answers, looking down.

"That sweet little old lady who makes the world's best milkshakes, is a fire elemental?"

"Yes, the strongest I know. She's the one who taught me to control my fire." I plop back on the couch.

"How the hell did I not feel her power?" Being a goddess, I should've sensed her a mile away.

"She's had many years to perfect her disguise." He moves closer to the door. "Coming?" he asks, looking back at me. "The store's open."

We lightly jog toward the village. Neither of us exerts much effort. Luckily, with the jog, it's difficult to talk. I'm not in the mood to carry on a conversation right now. The steeple comes into view, and the sun is high in the sky. As we enter the village, many people are milling around, completing their daily activities. "This place feels like home." It's the first thing Keegan's said since leaving the castle.

"I can understand why. It looks like a picture from a book." The old-fashioned soda fountain comes into view, and the neon open sign shines bright. Approaching the door, we see Brenna sitting behind the counter, reading a newspaper. A bell dings when Keegan enters.

"Keegan!" she exclaims, folding her paper and moving quickly toward us. "I was just thinking about you." She pulls him to a barstool. "Sit, sit. I'll make you your favorite."

"Brenna, this is..."

"I know who she is." The older woman interrupts while pouring a concoction of ice cream and ingredients together. "How is life in the castle, goddess?" she asks, handing Keegan his red milkshake.

Keegan and I make eye contact. "Good, I guess." My voice sounds weak. I reach out to her for any hints of her abilities and feel nothing. Everything about her feels human. "How are you hiding your energy from me?"

She smiles, handing me a blue milkshake identical to the first time we were here. "Drink up. I made it just for you." I stir my straw around, expecting something to jump out. "Don't worry your highness. I would never do anything to harm you." She smiles warmly.

We sit in silence, drinking our shakes while questions storm through my mind. Brenna picks up our empty mugs and drops them in the sink of water. She wrings her towel, wiping up a few drops of water off the bar. "My name is Brenna Erickson, and I was the first lesser Brigit ever created."

Holy shit. She just blurted that out. She shudders and her energy rushes me. Her power overflows, filling the store with her ability. Brenna smiles. "I'm guessing you're here because Keegan told you who I am, but I don't know what his purpose for doing that would be. Why don't you two fill me in on the details."

"In a nutshell, Astrid has killed Dagda and assembled an army at Castle Grimsgil." I stare at the woman, taking in all of her details. She looks to be in her late fifties. Her hair is turning white with age and her skin shows signs of sun throughout the years. Instead of copper, her eyes are pale blue.

Brenna smiles. "That little shit did it, didn't she?" She continues wiping the counter. "I couldn't stand that girl from the first minute I met her." She sits behind the bar. "So, Astrid has absorbed the powers of Dagda along with fire and has parked here in Iceland with the intention of killing you in revenge."

"Pretty much," Keegan answers.

"Without sounding harsh, I have to ask. Why are you here? I'm too old to fight her and to be honest, it's not my fight to enter." She looks around the store. "I've lived in this village since it was nothing more than a small settlement for the Norse. I don't have any desire to fight."

"I need you to train me," I blurt.

Brenna laughs. "Train you? You're the goddess of fire. Shouldn't you be doing the training?"

"In theory, yes." I scan her energy, deciding how much information I can divulge.

"I smell your power," she says, sniffing the air. "You are powerful."

"I've been told," I answer. "I need someone to help me master the element of fire. Keegan showed me how to start a fire, but I need more. I need to be able to do what I witnessed Brigit do. I need to become one with the flames."

Brenna sits quietly. She's studying every detail of my face and most likely my energy. "You're not telling me something."

"Can I trust you?" My voice is soft.

She sits up straight. "That's for you to decide. No one can tell you who you can and can't trust. Feel my energy. What does it tell you?"

"Llyr's my father."

"I know that, girl. You hold the power of water and fire."

I sigh. "Shu is my grandfather."

Brenna laughs deeply. "There it is. I knew there was something else." She slaps her hand on her knee. "Who knew Shu had it in him to reproduce? He's been drawn to humans of the male persuasion ever since I've known him."

I fight to keep my face neutral. How could I not have picked up on that? I clear my throat. "Will you train me or not?"

Brenna stands from her stool. "You hold the power of water, air, and fire yet don't know how to control any of them." Her words are not a question, but a statement. She's right.

I nod. "Will you help me?"

"How much time do we have?"

"To train?"

"Until she attacks?" she corrects.

I look down, linking my hands together. "We're not going to give her the chance."

She smiles. "Good. Tomorrow morning. I'll come to the castle. There's an entire wing that Brigit used for training and other nefarious deeds. We'll train there." I nod and follow Keegan out of the store. I feel her energy shield slip back in place, and the elemental power I felt minutes ago is gone, replaced by human energy.

"How did Rhys slip by Llyr and Shu?" Keegan asks on our walk back to the castle.

"That's a good question." I've wondered the same thing. Although, since I'm the goddess of fire, the more important question is how did Rhys slip by me. How did I not know who he was? Any feelings of grandeur I might have briefly held, have been washed away in one afternoon. The turret of the castle comes into view, and I feel a rush of energy immediately. Llyr and Shu are here. For the first time, I'm able to recognize them through their energy. I speed up, and Keegan stays right beside me.

"Is someone chasing us?" He turns to look behind, tripping over his foot and almost falling. I can't help but laugh at his clumsiness.

"No. Llyr and Shu are here." We round the corner into the courtyard.

"Did they send some sort of gods-only radar alert?"

"Maybe? I don't know how to explain it, but I know they're here." We run up the main stairs into the castle and straight into the office. I rush into Llyr's arms. "This sucks," I whisper into his shoulder.

"That it does." He wraps his arms around me. "We'll figure this out together. We're not leaving until we know you're safe."

Shu moves closer to us. "That bitch won't know what hit her."

"Murphy filled us in on the details. We offer every lesser at our disposal. There's no way Astrid can win if we combine." Llyr pulls away, keeping his arm around my shoulder. Shu moves toward me, giving me a brief hug. He's wearing a pair of white leather pants, sequin white shoes, and a white shirt covered in a pale blue paisley print. He looks handsome and savage all mixed together. I laugh thinking about Brenna's revelation. How could I have missed the signs?

"What?" he asks. "I didn't have time to dress properly." He motions to a wrinkle in the shirt. "This is what you get on last-minute notice."

"Thank you both for coming," I answer.

"We'd have it no other way," Shu says. "Who is this

lurking in the corner?" I turn to see Keegan standing wide-eyed and pressed far into the corner near the door.

Keegan steps forward. "Keegan Jacobson, your highness. I'm the chief of security. It's a pleasure to meet you both." He reaches his hand toward Llyr, who shakes it briefly. He does the same toward Shu who ignores the gesture.

"Seems to me the chief of security would've figured out who the goddess of fire has working for her." Shu takes another sip.

"Yes, sir. You are correct." Keegan retreats to his corner of safety.

"He was the one who figured it out," I answer. Shu still doesn't look convinced. "Keegan's not to blame. I should've done more research on him. I trusted him blindly. If you want to blame anyone, blame me."

"There's no one to blame. What's done is done. We need to focus on Astrid and how to overtake Castle Grimsgil before she discovers we're coming." Llyr turns to me. "What are the chances that another of her army is here?" He looks around the room.

"I'd say there's a big chance of that," Shu answers.

I sit on the couch. "I don't know. I researched everyone when we arrived and met with all the lessers, but still, Rhys slipped through the cracks. Can I say with one hundred percent accuracy that there are no more monster lessers here? No."

Murphy walks into the room dressed in full training gear. "Is something going on?"

"No, but I've taken the liberty to announce a mandated training session for all lessers living in or near the castle this evening." He moves toward Llyr. "Thank you for coming, Sires." He bows deeply to the gods. Murphy turns toward me. "Adria, someone wants to meet you, in person."

"Okay, who?"

On cue, a tall man wearing matching gear to Murphy walks into the office. His hair is so yellow it looks like it was colored with the brightest crayon in the box. His skin is dark and in perfect contrast to his vivid green eyes. The man falls to his knees. "My queen," his deep voice resonates throughout the room.

Llyr puts a hand on the man's shoulder. "Tempest. It's good to see you, my friend." I look at Murphy, raising my forehead in question. Murphy nods, confirming my suspicion.

Tempest stands and bows his head toward me. "I took you up on your invitation, my queen. How can I be of service?"

CHAPTER 8

*T*empest, the first water elemental I met, is here, standing in my office. Emotions overwhelm me, and I can't control the tears. Everyone in this room is here for me. I grew up alone, fighting to survive with no one to depend on but myself. My life has taken a full one-hundred-and-eighty-degree turn. I'm not alone anymore. This is what family feels like.

"I don't know how to thank you all." My words are swallowed by tears.

"You can stay alive," Shu answers, moving toward a large table. "It might be a good idea for everyone to get their thoughts on the same path." He pulls out a chair and sits gracefully. "Adria, call this meeting to order."

"Agreed," Llyr answers, pulling a chair out for me. The six of us sit around the large conference table for the next hour. Just as Murphy suggested, Shu agrees to send out a few hundred of his best lessers to spy on Castle Grimsgil. Together, we set a timeline of five days until we attack. Five days to bring every water, air, and willing fire elemental to the castle to fight for our survival. My human ego tells me there's no way in hell this is going to work.

"Have you mastered any of your elements?" Shu asks the million-dollar question.

"No," I answer honestly. "I can start a fire, but that's about it."

Keegan speaks for the first time. "Brenna is coming tomorrow to train her." At the mention of her name both Llyr and Shu look up.

"Brenna?" Llyr asks. "I thought she was dead."

"She's alive and well and makes a killer milkshake." I smile at the irony.

"She's agreed to train you to control fire?" Shu doesn't look convinced.

"I'm taking from your questions, that you two know her." I fold my arms in front of my chest.

"You could say that," Shu answers. "Like Llyr, I thought she died a few millennia ago." He laughs. "Hell, I can't believe Brigit didn't kill her."

"She raised me," Keegan says, drawing Llyr's attention.

"As a parent?" he asks.

"Sort of, yes. It was more like I moved in and never left. She didn't have a choice." Keegan stumbles over his words.

"Brenna always has a choice," Llyr answers. He looks at me. "She's the closest thing to Brigit with her powers. If she's agreed to train you, she's an asset to our team."

A small group of fire elementals in the courtyard

catches my eye. "Are they here for training?" I ask Murphy.

"Aye. I was hoping there'd be more." He stands. "Tempest, care to join me?"

"It'll be my pleasure." He grins a crooked grin.

"We're training them, Tempest. Not killing them," Murphy adds, making Tempest laugh.

"I'll be gentle." His deep voice vibrates throughout the room. Tempest's energy is calm, and I enjoy being around him. "Your Highnesses." He bows, following Murphy out of the room.

Shu sighs loudly. "When Brenna arrives, I think it best for Llyr and me to be with you. It's not that I distrust her as much as I want to annoy her with my presence."

"Sounds entertaining." I laugh. "Keegan, will you join me outside for training?"

"Yes, ma'am. I'll be outside." He stands. "Your Highnesses, it was a pleasure to meet you both." He bows awkwardly before exiting the room.

"He reminds me of the nerdy guy from *Friends*. You know, that television show that took place in a coffee shop," Shu says, watching Keegan leave the room.

"Ross?" I ask.

"Yes! That's the one. Am I the only one who sees the similarity? Well, maybe not in his looks, but the way he speaks in circles and confusion." He stands. "Llyr and I will find our rooms. Go train. Don't be surprised if this office is re-decorated when you get back." He looks around in disgust.

"That reminds me, some of the items we ordered have

arrived." His eyes light up at the news. "In that case, things will definitely look different when you return."

Llyr moves toward me. "We'll be with you every step of the way. I won't let anything happen to you." His words threaten to bring tears.

"I know." I kiss him on the cheek. "I'll let you know when Brenna arrives."

"Oh, don't worry. Believe me, we'll know." Shu answers while rearranging small dragons on one of the bookshelves.

......

I've been watching Tempest and Murphy from across the courtyard. Their body language is relaxed and comfortable, making me smile. Keegan joined them an hour or so ago, and the three of them have been working with the small group of fire elementals that showed up. They resemble an alternate universe version of the three stooges.

Instead of physical training, I've been working on controlling fire. So far, I've started a few small grass fires but nothing substantial. The sun has been low in the sky for several hours, and training is beginning to wind down. The three stooges work their way toward me. Tempest is at least half a foot taller than Murphy and Keegan, which means he's at least seven feet tall. The three of them side by side look like a terrifying defensive line. Tempest drops to one knee in front of me.

"My queen." He bows his head.

"Please stand, Tempest. As much as I appreciate the gesture, it's not necessary to bow to me. I'm just Adria." I place my hand on his shoulder as he looks up.

"You're more than that, my queen." He stands, towering over me.

"Adria, please." My voice sounds sad, even to me.

"Adria," he repeats, with a nod of his head.

Keegan moves toward Tempest. "I'll show the big guy to his quarters."

"That would be helpful. Thank you, Keegan." I smile a weak smile and watch the two of them walk away. They seem to have made fast friends, and I'm grateful.

"Let's go for a walk," Murphy says, leading me away from the castle. We don't speak, just walk around the perimeter, reminding me of our first night at Llyr's castle. I lean into him fully as we walk to the highest point on the castle grounds. The sun is disappearing behind the mountains, casting a shadowy glow through the land.

"I'm in over my head," I whisper. "I don't want to do this anymore. I miss being naive to this world."

"I'm so sorry, Adria." Murphy pulls me close, wrapping his arms around me, sharing the warmth of his energy through his touch. Several minutes pass before he speaks again. "You are the strongest person I know. You have the most powerful beings on the planet willing to die for you." He puts a finger under my chin, pulling my face toward his. "You're going to win this. *We're* going to win this." Gods, I love this man. He leans down, kissing my forehead as his energy calms the turmoil in my soul.

Murphy spends the night in my room, and I'm grateful for the company and the ability to not have to carry on a conversation. He knows what I need without me asking, and right now I don't need to be alone.

"What time did Brenna say she'd be here?" he asks, following me down the stairs. We're both dressed in full training gear.

"Brenna doesn't seem like the type that gives an exact time. She kind of moves when she wants."

"That's an understatement," Shu says from the bottom of the stairs. He and Llyr are waiting for us, both wearing similar gear to ours. Of course, Shu's gear is white, and I swear it shimmers in the light.

"It was stuck to the chicken's foot!" Keegan exclaims as he and Tempest exit the dining room. Both erupt into laughter. "Oh, Your Highnesses," Keegan says, bowing. "I didn't realize you were all out here." He stands awkwardly.

A knock on the door saves Keegan from himself. "Please, allow me." Shu moves toward the door. "Someone take a picture of her face when I open it." Keegan grabs his phone and is ready for the shot. I can't help but laugh at the irony of the entire situation. Shu slowly opens the door, making sure to give Keegan full access to Brenna's face for the photo.

"Well, shit," Brenna says just as the camera flash lights up the foyer. "They'll let anyone in here."

"Brenna. It's so good to see you again," Shu says, offering a side hug.

"I wish I could say the same," she counters. "Keegan, why are you taking pictures of me?" He shrugs, hiding his phone in his pocket.

"I'm going to need you to airdrop that to me later,"

Shu whispers before turning back to Brenna. "So, what have you been up to for the past few million years? I thought Brigit killed you." Shu is nothing but straight forward.

Brenna closes the door behind her. "She certainly tried a few hundred times." She laughs. "Guess these old bones still have some ability left in them."

Llyr steps toward the older woman. "Brenna, thank you for being here."

"I'm not doing it for you," she says. "I'm here for Adria and my element."

I step forward. "Thank you." She returns my smile.

"The rest of you are not invited. You can find something else to do with your time." Brenna gives an order to the crowd. No one moves. "You heard me. Get." She motions her arms like she's shooing away a herd of stray cats.

"I'll be okay," I reassure my family. "Go train. Brenna's taking me to the training wing of the castle." No one moves.

"Seriously?" Brenna asks the group. "If I meant her any harm, do you think I would've waited until the gods of water and air were in the same building? I see you two haven't changed a bit."

Llyr clears his throat loudly. "No, you wouldn't." He looks around the room. "Tempest and anyone else who wants to train, come with me to the courtyard."

Thank you. I mouth to my father. I squeeze Murphy's hand. "I'll see you at lunch."

"No, you won't," Brenna says. "We're training until dark, and I'll be sleeping here tonight." She looks at Shu.

"You're paying my employee to work in my store for as long as I'm here." She doesn't give him time to respond. "Adria will be staying with me in the training wing for the next few days."

"What the bloody hell?" Murphy asks.

"If you want me to train her, she'll need to be away from all other elements. Any interference from air or water will only hinder her control of fire." She looks each one of them in the eye. "Keegan, and only Keegan, will bring our meals and be allowed in that wing of the castle."

"You haven't changed a bit," Shu announces.

"I see you still wear sequins."

"Jealous much?" Shu laughs.

I put my hands up. "Enough. I will do what Brenna wants. I trust her." Murphy gives me a side eye, and I know he's thinking of my trust for Rhys that didn't pan out very well. "Do what she says. Keegan is the only one allowed in. I trust the rest of you to figure out the details of our plan while I'm gone. We don't have much time." All five men look at the floor like children being scolded. "I know you all have my best interest at heart, and I love you for it. But I must do this. You have to trust me."

"Dammit, Adria," Murphy whispers before closing his eyes in defeat.

"Good. That was lesson number one." Brenna says, moving toward the stairs. "You're in control, period." I follow her up the stairs to the unknown wing of the castle, feeling five pairs of eyes on my back the entire climb.

"Don't turn around," Brenna whispers. "They're still staring. It'll do them some good to learn their place in your life. You are the goddess, not them. They need to look at you as their equal, not some child they must protect."

I do what she says, following her in the opposite direction of mine and Murphy's rooms in the castle. She leads me down a long hall until the tapestries that are prevalent throughout the castle change style and look much older. The red carpet turns into older pine flooring, and the lighting turns into old oil lanterns. "I've never been in this area."

"You wouldn't have." Brenna opens a much smaller door. "Brigit shut this part off years ago."

I follow her through the door, ducking to keep from bumping my head. "Why are you bringing me here?"

"Much the same reason your grandfather insisted on opening the door for me. To piss them off." She huffs a laugh. "The training facility in this area is old and out of date but was built not to burn. The entire castle could burn, and this wing will be untouched."

"In other words, I won't burn the castle down from here."

"Bingo," she answers. "It's not much further." Her voice is warm and soothing. "Thank you for trusting me." We turn another corner and to an even smaller door. Brenna leads us inside and pulls a flashlight out of her bag. "There's a generator in that corner." She points her light to the back of a large, windowless room. "Take my light and see if you can get it started. There's electricity in here once you get it going. I'll find the switches."

Just like she said, a large red box sits in the back corner. The machinery looks no older than a year or two. "It's solar-powered," she says from the other side of the room. There's a panel on the outside of the wall that's powered by the sun.

"That's kind of smart."

"Brigit had her moments." Brenna laughs. A large black switch on the front of the box reads "on/off." Would it be that simple? I flip the switch on and the box roars to life. The hum of the generator isn't as loud as I expected.

The room lights up, revealing a large square that resembles an ancient ballroom. "There we go," Brenna says with a smile.

The floors are wooden and ancient. Deep scratches, some resembling claw marks, cover the antique birch. Ornate blue wallpaper lines the walls topped with lavish gold woodwork. Scorch marks on the ceilings show evidence of fires from years past. "What is this room?"

"It's been the training room for the past few hundred years. This is part of the original castle built by the Norse around the turn of the century. The wood in these floors came from their ships." I bend down, rubbing my fingers through a particularly deep groove.

"They're strangely beautiful," I whisper. "Are these claw marks?"

Brenna follows my line of sight and shrugs, completely unfazed. "Probably. Who knows?" She moves toward a door that leads off the main room. "Here's where you'll be sleeping." The door opens, revealing a small room containing a bed and mirror. The covers are new and fresh.

"How's this possible?" I ask, running my hands across the white comforter.

"I have my ways," she answers. "My room is on the other side." She points to an identical door opposite mine.

"Brenna, if you want me to continue trusting you, I need to know how you managed to have this room in this ancient part of the castle clean and ready to sleep in without anyone knowing or seeing you. I know you had help, and I know it wasn't Keegan. He couldn't pull this off without awkwardly announcing what he was doing the entire time. Who did this?"

She sighs. "Fair enough. I don't think you're going to like my answer." She shifts from foot to foot. If I didn't know better, I'd say she was nervous. "I have a connection inside the castle." I wait patiently for her revelation. "Rhys."

CHAPTER 9

*B*renna's right. I don't like her answer. Energy coils at my core, ready for whatever might happen. "Rhys?" I repeat.

She sighs, sitting on an old Victorian-style couch in the corner of the room. "There'll be no need for all that." She circles a crooked finger at my core. "I promised you could trust me, and I mean that. I'm not dumb enough to think I could defeat you in a battle, not that I would engage in such childishness." She pats the empty spot next to her. "Join me, and I'll explain."

"I'd prefer to stay here." My words are short and clipped.

Brenna picks at a loose string on the couch. "Rhys and I are... seeing each other." I watch her twist the string between her thumb and finger. "We've been together for quite a while."

"You and Rhys are... dating?" This conversation took a totally different turn than I expected.

"I'm not sure at our age dating is the right word, but we're a couple and have been for a few decades."

"He was in prison before I asked you to train me. He wouldn't have been able to get this done."

"He's had the room ready since the first time we met."

"When Keegan brought us there for milkshakes?" I ask.

"I knew who you were the moment you walked in. I also knew you needed help, and it wouldn't be long before Keegan would tell you who I really am. He's not the best at keeping secrets." She pauses. "You don't live as long as I have without seeing things that aren't always right in front of us."

I lean against the wall, propping one boot on the ancient wallpaper. "Do you know *what* Rhys is?" My lip curls at the memory of the photo Keegan showed.

"I do." She scoots forward. "He's changed." Before I can argue, she continues. "Believe me, I know how cliché that sounds. But it's true. He's no longer one of those... those vile creations of Brigit's." I try to keep my face neutral as Brenna sighs. "He came to me looking for an escape. I was shocked that he found me. I'd been hiding under her filthy nose for centuries, and she had no clue."

"She didn't know you lived in the village?" I ask, wrinkling my forehead.

Brenna laughs. "Not one damn clue. Brigit had her head so far up her ass, I could've lived in the room next to hers, and she probably wouldn't have noticed. Her life revolved around her children and defeating your father. She's wanted his power since the beginning of time." I remember Llyr saying something similar.

"You hid your energy from her?"

"Of course. I'm not an idiot. The same way I hid it from you."

I slide my boot off the wall. "Can you teach me to do that?"

Brenna scratches her head. "Probably. Keegan learned."

"You taught Keegan to hide his power? Who would he need to hide from?"

She sighs. "Brigit. If he told you who I am, no doubt he told you he lived here, at the castle." I nod. "When he escaped, he needed to be able to hide his energy when I wasn't around."

"Tell me why I should trust Rhys." I change the subject.

She pauses. "That's not why we're here."

"Agreed, but if you can help Rhys, I need you to try. I need a reason to get him out of that prison."

She stands. "The reason we're in this castle, hidden away from your father, grandfather, and that hunky British hybrid is the exact reason I won't defend him. You don't need another person making decisions for you. They do it in the name of love and keeping you safe, but they're hurting you. They're pulling your power away by not giving you the power you've earned and deserve." Brenna steps closer. "You are the goddess of fire, water, and air. While Llyr and Shu live, your power in their elements is weaker, second only to theirs."

Anger fills me. "What are you telling me?"

"As much as they annoy me, I have nothing but respect for both, even Shu and his damn sequins." She moves a few feet in front of me. "Adria, you have to stop letting them control you. You must step into your power and become what Astrid can't, the goddess of all elements." I stare into her pale blue eyes.

"You're telling me to forget my human side and become fully elemental." I fight tears. "I've heard it all before."

"Quite the opposite, my girl. I'm telling you to embrace who you are. Every aspect, even the human part, makes you who you are." She pauses. "You are literally the perfect creation and combination of every living thing on this planet. That's how you will defeat Astrid. That's how we will win this useless war."

Her words knock the wind from my lungs. I plop down on the couch. Brenna answered the unanswered questions that have plagued me since I first discovered who I am. We sit in silence for what feels like an eternity. I don't know how much time passes before she goes into her bedroom on the other side of the room. My mind is a mess of thoughts and feelings.

In a room with no windows, time isn't the same. Day and night don't exist, and I have no clue if we've been in here for one hour or twelve. A soft knock on the door brings me back to reality. I stand, watching the door creak open. "Hello?" Keegan whispers. "Brenna, Adria?"

"We're here," Brenna answers, coming out of her room. "Why are you here?" He walks in carrying a tray covered with food.

"Shu sent dinner."

"What time is it?" I ask.

He looks at his watch. "Seven thirty." He moves to the only table in the room and sets the tray on the corner.

Brenna takes the top off the plates. "This actually looks good. Did Shu cook it?"

Keegan laughs. "No, Tempest did."

"Well, then it's safe to eat." She laughs.

Keegan looks between the two of us. "Everything okay in here?"

I take a deep breath. "Yes, we're fine. Please tell Murphy I'm fine and to stop worrying."

He laughs. "I don't think he's going to listen."

"Make him listen." My words sound harsh.

"Yes, ma'am." Keegan turns to leave.

"Oh, Keegan." He turns. "Get Rhys out of that prison and into the planning of our mission to Castle Grimsgil."

"Are you sure that's a good idea?"

"Don't question me. Do as I ask. If anyone else disagrees with my decision, tell them to take it up with me when I return." Keegan stares at me, unsure what to say. "Thank you for bringing dinner." He doesn't move. "You may go." He doesn't waste a minute leaving the room. Footsteps sound like running as he moves away from the room.

"That's better," Brenna says.

"Me being a bitch is better?"

"No, you being in control is better. There's a fine line between being a bitch and being in control. Being a woman makes that line even more difficult. You weren't a bitch. You gave him orders and asked him to carry them out." She sets the plates on the table. "This smells wonderful. Little known fact, Shu is an amazing cook. I'm going to guess he helped Tempest a little."

"My guess is he's redecorating."

Brenna laughs. "That too. He's quite extravagant but he's good at heart. We may goad each other and truthfully, I'd be worried if he was nice to me, but he's someone who I trust completely. He would die for you. They both would."

"I don't want them to."

"That's why we're here. Controlling your element is ninety-nine percent mental and one percent skill. Your mind is holding you back." She takes a bite of the pasta Keegan brought. "Come, sit, and eat. I know Firsts don't eat much, but this was made with love, and it tastes like it."

I sit beside her, moving the food around on my plate. "You know what's ironic?" Brenna raises her eyebrows in question. "The old Adria wouldn't have thought twice about telling Keegan where to go and how long it should take him to get there. I was a bitch with a capital B. Now, I'm riddled with guilt that I hurt his feelings."

Brenna laughs. "Keegan grew up around me. If he can survive that without hurt feelings, you telling him what to do didn't faze him."

My fork clunks loudly on the plate. "How do I step into my power? You're not the first person to tell me that was the answer, but no one seems to give any clues on exactly how to achieve it."

She turns toward me with a smile. "You have to believe it."

"I do." The look on her face says she doesn't believe me. "No, really. I do." Dammit, she's right, I don't.

"Tell me about your life." I watch her stack the plates, scrapping what's left of the meal into a napkin.

I sit back in the chair. "You sure you want to know?" I try laughing off the awkwardness. She doesn't respond. "Okay, here's the abridged version. I grew up a proud member of the California foster care system, joined the military as soon as I was old enough only to avoid a prison sentence for grand theft auto, and was recruited into the Phoenix unit to train humans to fight the lower lesser elementals, watched my friends die, watched my best friend die, and watched myself slowly dying on the inside. I didn't care who I hurt, didn't take care of myself, didn't care about anything." My words decrescendo the longer I talk. "That was my life until Murphy showed up, and I'm pretty sure you know the rest."

Brenna's eyes soften. "Sweet girl. You just identified your demons. The only person holding you back is your-self. You don't believe you are worthy." Tears instantly flow. "All those things that hurt you when you were young. Everything you've been through since birth has made you stronger. The things we experience aren't always meant to scar us for life. Yes, they leave a mark, but those marks heal over time. It's when they become scars that they give us our strength and power. Don't hide the pain of your life. Use it to make you stronger. Pull on its power to fuel your strength. Those scars are your strength."

I stare at the woman in front of me. She gently wipes a tear from my cheek. I grab her hand before she has a chance to lower it, holding it in mine. "Thank you." My words are inadequate, but they're all I can say.

"Get some rest. We'll train tomorrow." I do as told and move into my small room. The three-drawer dresser beside the bed is stocked with clothes in my size. Dammit, Rhys. I pull out a set of sleep shorts and a matching tank top and slip into the comfort of familiarity. Sleep comes quickly and I'm grateful.

"Adria?" a soft voice echoes through my mind. "Adria. Get your ass up."

I sit up in bed. "Hannah?" She sits on the edge of the mattress wearing her signature holy jeans and alien hoodie.

"Yep. Miss me?"

"Gods, yes. I need you so much right now." I stare at my dead best friend.

Her voice loses its teasing tone. "That's why I'm here. I told you I'd be here as long as you need me."

"Tell me what to do."

"No," she answers. "Brenna was right. You're the only thing holding you back. No one can tell you what to do or how to fix it, but you."

"If we attack, will people die?"

Hannah takes my hand into hers. "You already know that answer."

"I can't order people to their deaths."

"If you don't, you condemn the entire world to death."

I pull my hand away. "Are you saying if we don't order the attack at Grimsgil I'm putting a world full of humans at risk?"

"Astrid's not going to stop here. If you give her the

chance to attack, she'll kill you, Shu, and Llyr. She'll assume your powers and won't stop until the entire world is hers. Unlike you, she won't care who she kills. You have no choice." Hannah looks down.

"What aren't you telling me?"

"People you love will die."

"Hannah. Who will die?"

She pauses. "I've seen it, but you have to know our world is full of endless possibilities. There are many possible outcomes, I've seen only one."

"Who will die?"

She stands. "I've said too much. It's forbidden to share details like that with you."

"Forbidden? By whom?"

"Brenna will help you. Do what she says. Step into your power and change the timeline. Make your own ending." With her words, she disappears.

"Hannah!" I yell into the darkness.

The door to my room opens, revealing bad ceiling lights. "Talking to ghosts?" Brenna asks.

"Something like that."

"Let's get started." She opens the door wide. "You won't need that training suit you wore in here yesterday. I believe you'll find more appropriate clothing in the drawers." Just like she said, the bottom drawer is full of leggings and tank tops. I make a mental note to not only apologize to Rhys but give him a huge raise when we get through this.

Ten minutes later, Brenna is dressed much the same, standing in the center of the ballroom. "Fire isn't something that can be controlled. None of the elements can.

Elementals pretend to control them, but in truth, they aren't. The first step of control is knowing that you aren't in control." I step a few feet in front of her. "Take all of the pain, all of the joy, and all of the love you've held inside your entire life. Pull those emotions and use them to fuel your power. Wad them up into a little ball of fire and shape it to whatever you want." She points at a wooden box. "Make that box feel what you feel."

I don't know where to start. A few seconds in, the box begins to smoke.

"No," she says sternly. "That's not how a goddess controls her element. Try again." I try, and this time small flames form around the base. "No, you're not Keegan or a lesser. You're the damn goddess of fire. Burn that bitch into nothing more than ashes." Anger fills my soul as she scolds me for something I don't know how to do. "No," she demands. "Again." We repeat the same game back and forth for hours until I can't take it anymore.

"Shut up!" I scream. "I don't know what to do! I can't do what you want."

"Yes, you can." Her energy matches mine. "Do it now!" I try again and large flames shoot from the box. "Not good enough," she repeats. "Keegan can do better than that. Do you think Astrid is going to produce worthless flames when she comes after your family? Do you think she'll spare that man you love because she has a heart locked deep inside? Do you think she'll show you any form of sympathy as she absorbs and obliterates your kingdom and you? Take control, Adria. Use your power."

A rush of emotions flows from the depths of my soul. Pulling energy from the walls, the floor, the world outside, and from Brenna herself. I focus every bit on the box. In an instant the box explodes, the generator shuts off and the two of us are standing in total darkness.

"That's a start."

After the box explosion, Brenna retreats to her room, leaving me alone in the darkness. I spark a small flame, lighting a candle on the table. It gives enough light to see no further than ten feet in diameter, but it's all that I need. *Take Control* plays through my head on repeat. I've never been in control of any part of my life... even now. I decide to do something I haven't done in years. I meditate.

Out of all the foster homes I lived in as a kid, only a few were safe and comfortable. One of those, my host parent was a spiritual guru who insisted I learn to meditate. She would play music while the two of us sat quietly in a darkened room. At the time I thought she was crazy. I mostly played along because I liked her. Thinking back on the techniques she taught me, I find a spot on the floor and sit. Taking a few deep breaths in through my nose and out through my mouth, I allow my body and mind to relax. The quiet in the room becomes deafening. Water dripping from who knows where sounds like water rushing from a waterfall. Dust floating through the air makes tiny explosions as it hits the walls.

Concentrating on the monotony of the water drips, I allow my mind to float from this room to a world of pictures and memories. Images flash before my eyes in rapid succession, landing me in the middle of a room where I'm surrounded by toys. A toddler bed is to my left and a dresser with drawers hanging open on the right.

"Adria, come on baby. We're going to be late." A

woman calls from another room. "You better not be taking that bathing suit off again," she scolds. My memory floats into the same room as the voice.

The woman in front of me is tall with long, blonde hair tied into a bun. Her eyes are blue, and freckles line her cheeks. "There you are." She sighs. "Seriously, why are you holding your top?" She scoops me into her arms. "Never mind, we'll fix it when we get there." She wraps a beach towel around me, and we leave.

The next image is of blue water lapping against a beach. I'm sitting beside the woman, playing in the sand. "Don't get that sand in your eyes. It's a bitch to get out," she says with a smile.

"Claire, she's just a baby. She doesn't know what you're saying," a woman I don't recognize says.

Claire laughs. "Don't underestimate this one. She's special." She looks at me. "Aren't you, my love?" Her hand ruffles the top of my head. "I need to wash some of this sand off. Will you watch her for a minute?" she asks the stranger.

"Sure! Go catch some waves. I'll keep an eye on this special one." I watch Claire stand and head toward the water. She turns to wave and blows me a kiss.

"I'll be right back," she yells from the shoreline. I watch as she walks into the water until nothing but her head is showing.

"Not if things go the way they're supposed to, you won't," the stranger next to me says. She picks me up, moving closer to the water. "Look at Mama. She won't be there much longer."

Oh, my gods. This is the moment that Claire was

killed. I'm trapped in the body of a toddler and unable to do anything to stop it. I watch as Claire's blonde hair goes under the water and back to the top several times.

"Oops, I thought he had her that time. You need to watch this. I'm sorry you have to go through this, but your future has already been decided and Claire isn't part of it." She faces me toward my mother where I see her go under once more, this time she doesn't resurface. Tiny arms and legs flail in front of me, but the woman holds me tight. I turn toward the stranger. I just witnessed Claire drown and this woman planned it.

"You're too young to understand, but one day you will." She carries me to where our towels and clothes were left, gathering them into a bag. "I'll make sure you're taken care of and safe today. After that, the rest is up to you." She turns me toward her. "We will meet again one day, that I'm sure of. Today was the day I put that into motion. When the time is right, you'll understand."

"Who are you?" screams through my mind. I watch in horror as she takes me to a lifeguard, telling them the story of how she watched a stranger, my mother, walk into the water and never return. The man takes me and begins frantically calling for help. I watch the woman walk away, leaving me with lifeguards and a dead mother.

"Vita," whispers through my mind. "My name is Vita."

I jump to my feet, taking a minute to ground my body to this reality. "Brenna!" I call. She's in front of me in an instant.

"You okay?"

I walk in circles, running my hands through my hair.

"I don't know." I turn toward the generator, sending a shock of power straight into the machine. It roars to life and the lights return to their dim, creepiness. Brenna looks at me strangely but doesn't speak. "Who's Vita?"

She pulls a chair from under the table and sits down. "Now that's a name I haven't heard in a long while."

"Don't waste my time. Who's Vita?" For the first time, I feel in complete control of my words and actions.

"You might want to sit for this one." She sighs. I cross my arms on my chest and stare. "Or not." She clears her throat. "Vita is the fifth element."

I stare at her in confusion. "There are only four elements. Earth, water, air, and fire. What am I missing?"

"The fifth element is the element of aether or pure life. Vita is the essence of all First Elementals and is the purest of them all." Brenna's voice is soft, almost in awe. I pull a chair out, sitting next to her.

"There's a fifth element whose name is Vita and she's stronger than all four First Elementals combined?"

Brenna smiles. "Yes. did you see her?"

Sitting back in the chair. "Yes, but I think it was an accident. It was more like a memory. I didn't see her live."

"If you saw her, it wasn't an accident. You were meant to see her at this time in your life. What did she say?"

I think back on her words. "After she made me watch my mother drown, she told me we would meet again, and her drowning was the catalyst to set our future meeting into motion."

"What does that mean?" Brenna asks.

"How the hell am I supposed to know?" Words fly out of my mouth in anger.

"What did she look like?"

I wrinkle my forehead. "I don't know. Just a regular person. Brown curly hair and green eyes are all I remember. She looked like an ordinary person, enjoying a day at the beach."

"No one has seen her before. You're the first." Brenna is acting like a teenager talking about their first crush. She stands, moving closer. "Everything in your life has led up to his. That's why she allowed you to see her. That's why she chose this moment to reveal that memory to you." She pulls me up from the chair. "Burn it." She points to the table.

"What? After what I just told you, now's not the time for training. Give me a minute to get my thoughts together first."

"You don't need a minute. I feel it inside you. Burn it." I sigh, turning to the table. The thought doesn't even have to leave my mind before the table bursts into roaring flames. "Now, put it out." A mere thought and water rushes over the flames. She points to the far corner of the room. "Get rid of that wall." The thought barely flows before the entire back wall, holding the generator, explodes outward onto a long-forgotten courtyard below. Brenna smiles. "Just as I thought. You're in control."

The hallway door opens, revealing a nervous Keegan. "Did something just explode?" He walks into the room wearing what looks like a hazmat suit.

"What the hell are you wearing?" I ask with a smile.

"I call it my 'just in case' suit. It protects me from fire."

"Oh, dear gods. Keegan, you're a fire hybrid. Fire won't burn you," Brenna answers.

"Not the normal kind of fire." He carries a tray to the scorched and soaking wet table. "Let's just say I didn't want to look like this table or worse, that wall." The tray holds two plates and several bottles of water. "Shu made this meal, so I can't promise it's not poisoned. However, he didn't specify which plate went to which person, so I'm going to guess he wouldn't poison his granddaughter, which means it's safe for you to eat, Brenna."

"That was the longest sentence in history," she answers. "Thank you, and please tell Shu thank you."

"Yeah, okay." He laughs. "I don't think he'll believe the thank you came from you." He walks back to the door.

"Keegan?" I call after him. "We're finished here. Brenna and I will be back shortly. Tell the others we have much to talk about." He nods in understanding. "And you can take that suit off. I promise you're safe." I watch him back his way through the door, afraid to turn his back on us, closing the door behind him.

"That boy is a mess," Brenna says with a laugh. I pick up an extra crispy piece of bacon, relishing the crunch in my mouth.

"This is actually good." I end up eating four pieces before Brenna eats one. "Why did his grandmother give up on him?"

"That's a tough question. She's human, and although she didn't understand how, I think she knew he started the fire at the cottage. She provided a home but no love. He found his way to me, and I'm glad he did. He's a good boy, and I think of him as a son, or I guess grandson." She laughs. "Despite his awkwardness, he's the smartest person I've ever met and the perfect addition to your team."

"I couldn't agree more," I answer, finishing off the last of her bacon.

CHAPTER 10

I follow Brenna through the ancient halls until the decor begins to look more modern. I half expected Murphy to be waiting in the wings for our return. Honestly, I'm glad he's not. That means he's doing what I asked and getting our attack situated.

We reach the top of the stairs and surprisingly, the entire castle is silent. "Where are they?" Brenna asks.

"Preparing for battle." We enter my office and I'm in shock. Yesterday when we left, the room was several shades of red complete with horrible decorations. Today, the walls are a soft gray color, the decor is clean and modern, and it feels like home.

"Looks like Shu's been here," Brenna says with a laugh.

"It's beautiful." I run my hands across the small wooden desk that sits where a once gigantic monstrosity was.

"Thank you," Shu says from the door. "It was a labor of love. I *loved* watching the workers *labor*."

"I bet you did," Brenna mumbles.

Looking around the room, I try to take in everything. "This is perfect." I move toward him and wrap my arms around his small frame. Shu hugs me back and adds a few pats on my back.

"I'm glad you like it." He pulls away, looking between the two of us. "Well, did Brenna corrupt you? Did you find out all her secrets?" He moves to the couch, patting a space beside him. "Sit and spill the beans. Tell me all that old hags secrets."

"You do know I'm in the same room?" Brenna asks.

Shu looks up, acting surprised. "Oh, I didn't see you there." He smiles a fake smile.

"Brenna helped me quite a lot," I answer.

"You helped yourself," she corrects. "I just talked some sense into you."

Thoughts of Vita come to mind. "Where is everyone? I need to catch up on what's been done here."

Shu stands. "Well, the young ones have been recruiting, training, and preparing for battle while Llyr and I do what we do best."

"Walk around and look busy?" Brenna asks.

Shu ignores her. "I've sent spies in all directions of Grimsgil from the air and Llyr has done the same by water."

I scrunch my eyebrows. "Grimsgil isn't by the sea."

"No, my girl, it isn't. But the mountains surrounding it are covered in snow." Llyr walks into the room and I move quickly to his side. "Shu used his wind to blow a few of my smaller lessers onto parts of the castle. Water vapor is still water."

"Oh, that's genius." Why didn't I think of that earlier?

"I'm expecting a report back within the hour. How did it go in there? I sense a change in you." Llyr pulls away from me. He looks at Brenna. "Thank you." She nods in response. "What happened?"

I take a deep breath. "Brenna was helpful, but my breakthrough came when I meditated." Both gods stare at me without interruption. I sigh, not really sure how to talk about Claire to Llyr and Shu. "You guys might want to sit down for this." They take opposite ends of the couch looking very opposite in space and looks. I lean against the edge of my new desk. "When I meditated, I was transported back to a memory of being a toddler." I pause. "The day Claire died." I look at both of them, not sure how they're going to handle this information. Llyr nods, giving me silent permission to continue.

"We were in a small apartment, and I was dressed to go to the beach. Claire was fussing at me for taking my bathing suit off." Llyr chuckles but doesn't interrupt. "The next scene, we were transported to the beach. I was playing in the sand while she was talking to a woman that we met there. They seemed like they knew each other, like they were friends." My arms cross in front of my chest. "The two of them talked while I did typical toddler things next to them. Claire said she wanted to wash the sand off and asked the woman to watch me while she did." I find a chip in the wood floor to focus on before continuing. "I saw her moving further into the water and watched her go under a few times. The stranger picked me up and took me to the shoreline so I could watch what was about to happen."

"This woman knew Claire was about to drown and wanted you to watch?" Shu interrupts.

I nod. "She told me my future had already been decided, and Claire wasn't part of it." I turn to Llyr. He has tears in his eyes. The god of the sea has tears in his eyes. "I'm so sorry," I whisper. He closes his eyes and nods.

"Me too. Please go on," he whispers back.

"After she, after she... drowned, the woman handed me to a lifeguard, telling them she'd seen a woman go into the water and leave me on the beach." Where Llyr's sad, Shu is pissed.

"So, this woman knew Claire was going to drown and most likely orchestrated the whole thing?" He stands from the couch.

"I think so," I answer.

Shu walks across the room and kicks a soft pillow on the ground. "We need to find out who she is. *I* need to find out who she is." Llyr sits in silence, saying more than words ever could.

"She told me Claire's death would put in motion the two of us meeting again, and one day I would understand why it had to happen." Neither god speaks. "That memory released my powers."

"The memory of Claire's, of your mother's death, opened your abilities fully?" Shu asks. I nod in response.

"I always knew her death wasn't a freak accident by one of my lessers, but this isn't what I expected. Hell, I don't know what I expected." Llyr runs his hands through his blonde hair, reminding me very much of a human action. "Who's this woman that's responsible for Claire's death? I want her name." Llyr's body language has changed.

"We can fight over who gets vengeance," Shu says.

"Was it Brigit?" Llyr moves toward Brenna.

"Don't be daff, Llyr. Brigit was crazy, but even she wouldn't sink to that depth." Brenna turns toward me. "Maybe you should ask your daughter who the woman was."

"Vita. The woman was Vita." My words stop Llyr in his tracks.

Both Llyr and Shu look at me like I spoke a foreign language. "Vita?" Shu repeats. "Vita arranged for Claire's death so the two of you would meet again one day. Why would she do that?"

"Because she's just like the stories paint her, a vindictive bitch who wants to control every element in this realm," Brenna adds.

Llyr looks at me. "I've always believed the stories of Vita were just tales, passed down over the millennia. Are you sure it was Vita? The real Vita? It could've been someone pretending to be Vita, using her name."

"Vita's real," Shu says softly. "We've met several times throughout the years." Every eye in the room turns toward him. "I know what you're thinking, Llyr. No, I had nothing to do with Claire's death. I haven't seen Vita for a millennia or two."

"Why would you meet with Vita?" Llyr's voice is low and precise.

Shu shrugs. "She showed up at my home a few times. She didn't really say anything important, just would stay there for days on end then disappear as mysteriously as she arrived." He opens a cart in the corner of the room, revealing a hidden wine bar, and pours a huge glass of brandy. "She scared the shit out of me, so I entertained her, told her enough to keep her guessing, and turned on the charm until she left." He drinks half the glass in one gulp.

"You didn't think this was important enough to share with the rest of the Firsts?" Llyr asks.

"At the time, no."

Llyr moves closer to Shu and the energy in the room becomes palpable. "You didn't think holding private meetings with the goddess of all elementals was something that you might want to share? She's pure energy, Shu. She makes the Firsts look like lower-level lessers in comparison."

"Stop!" I walk between the two gods. "Enough, both of you." Shu drinks the rest of his brandy. "What's done is done. Right now, our focus needs to be on Astrid and the hoard at Grimsgil. Whatever Vita's plan is, or was, doesn't affect the fact that we now have less than three days before we attack."

I focus all my energy and in a split second, I'm floating in the air engulfed by flames. "That memory helped me. Yes, the memory sucked, but it unlocked something that's been hiding deep inside since then." Using air, I lift Shu and Llyr to my level. "I have full control over water, air, and fire." Both gods lower their eyes. "We will win this battle." My words echo through the room as the three of us hang in midair.

The door to the office opens, revealing the rest of our

battle party. Tempest and Rhys immediately bow to one knee, while Murphy stares in awe. I release the energy holding us in place and the fire recedes from around me. "Dammit, Tempest! I need my suit," Keegan says, stepping from behind Murphy.

Murphy moves quickly to my side. "Are you okay?" he whispers, inches in front of me.

"I'm okay." I smile with my answer.

"Looks like you might have mastered a few things while you were gone." He moves closer.

Shu clears his throat loudly. "I think I speak for everyone in this room when I say, please don't kiss right now." Murphy looks down with a smile. I turn to the men still bowing to me.

"Please stand up, gentlemen." Rhys barely comes to Tempest's shoulder. In his defense, he doesn't look down as I approach him. "Rhys, I owe you an apology. I hope you understand the reasoning for our rash decision and will join us as we fight against them now."

"Your Highness, I mean, Adria, there's nothing to forgive. You did what you thought was best, and any leader would've done the same." He takes my hand into his, kissing the back. "I pledged my allegiance to you the first moment we met and that pledge still remains. I will fight to the death with you and for you. I'm no longer one of them."

"Thank you." I move toward Tempest, stretching high on my tiptoes, I wrap my arms around his muscular neck. "You are a blessing to me and our entire group. I'm so happy you took me up on the invitation to join us from the sea." Tempest looks down and I watch a tear slide down his cheek. I move closer to Keegan. "You are strong, brave, and a goofball, and I'm grateful you decided to move back to Iceland to be with us." Out of the corner of my eye, Brenna shifts her weight from one foot to the other. "You are very loved and appreciated."

The men in front of me all stare at me with solemn looks. "What happened in there?" Murphy asks. "Are you sure you're okay?"

"I'm better than okay. I'm complete." I lace my fingers through his and pull him toward the large conference table. The bulky office chairs have been replaced with simple, plush bean bag style chairs and the table lowered to match. I look around the table of eight. "Tell me what's been done."

Murphy is the first to speak. "We've gathered over six hundred lessers that are willing to fight Astrid."

"Fire?" I ask.

"Most, a few hundred are water who were close by," Tempest answers. "Combined with the air and water that are already at Grimsgil, we have almost a thousand."

"Will that be enough?" Brenna asks.

"It'll have to be," Llyr answers.

"Shu, what have your spies reported?" I ask.

He sighs before answering. "Between the monster fire lessers and earth lessers, they number over two thousand."

"Shit. That's two for every one of us," I whisper.

"Yes, but the three of you," Keegan says, pointing to Llyr, Shu, and me, "make that a pretty even score. Adria should count for at least a thousand on her own."

"Ross has a point," Shu answers. "Astrid holds the

power of two elements, but does she have full control?" I hide my smile at Shu's name for Keegan.

"My spies say, yes," Llyr answers.

"If I might?" Rhys raises a hand. "I have first-hand knowledge of the castle and grounds. What you're seeing from above is just a small portion of what could be hiding below. There could be hundreds more hiding out of sight."

"Well, shit," Shu says, filling another glass. "Have any more great news to share?"

"Yes, actually. There are miles of tunnels underground that connect the castle to the sea," Rhys adds.

"To the sea?" Llyr questions.

"Yes. Most of them were flooded and blocked by Brigit, but one was left open as a last-resort escape route. That tunnel leads straight into the main courtyard of the castle and to Brigit's chambers."

"That's the answer. That's our way into the castle," Tempest says.

"I agree, but Brigit made sure it was flooded at all times. She believed it kept the regular fire lessers from being a threat," Rhys continues.

"Then we fly in." Shu slides forward in his bean bag. "I'll call all my lessers to me. Hell, I could fly half of them in on my own."

"Murphy and I will take care of getting the water lessers inside through the tunnel. We'll attack from inside while air attacks from out." Llyr copies Shu's movement in the chair.

"No one is allowed near Astrid, but me," I demand.

"Did you forget she's the only one who can kill you?" Llyr asks.

"That's precisely the reason I'm the only one who will go near her." I look at the two gods. "She's more powerful than both of you."

"Whatever happened in that room, made you a little bossy," Shu says, looking me up and down. "Besides, she doesn't scare me."

"She should," Brenna says. "That girl's crazy. She'll kill anyone she sees."

I stand from the chair. "Maybe Shu's right. I am being a little bossy." I look between the two of them. "You both said it's time to step into my powers." Shu looks me in the eyes. "This is me doing that."

"I'll follow you to the ends of the earth and beyond," Shu answers. "I kind of like being told what to do for a change." He laughs. "But only by you. Don't get any bright ideas, Llyr." He points a slender finger toward my father who holds up both hands in surrender style.

Shu's words lighten the mood, slightly. "It's settled then. Murphy, Tempest, and Llyr will lead the water lessers through the tunnel. Shu and I, along with air lessers, will fly the fire lessers into the castle. Once inside, we leave no one alive."

CHAPTER 11

*M*urphy and I sit opposite each other on the couch in my room. "I don't like being separated from you during the battle." His words are soft.

"I'm not a fan either, but I don't see any other way. It's going to take all three of you to lead the lessers through that tunnel." Lying down, I put my head on his thigh, lacing my fingers through his.

"What happened in there, with Brenna? What did she do that Llyr and Shu couldn't?" His thumb rubs slow circles on the back of my hand.

"It wasn't Brenna," I answer. "Well, she pissed me off enough to make me seek answers, so maybe it was her." I laugh awkwardly. "I had a vision."

Murphy's thumb stops moving. "Like the one of the castle?"

I sit up, facing him. "It was more of a memory than a vision." I pause. "I saw Claire's death." For the first time today, I let the emotion of everything overwhelm me, and

I fight to speak. "I saw what happened, that day. The day she drowned."

Murphy pulls me close. "I'm so sorry."

I snuggle close. "Me too. Oh, I almost forgot. Thank you for letting Rhys out. I wasn't sure you'd believe Keegan."

He laughs, deeply. "It took him a while, but he finally convinced Tempest and me the order was from you."

"Do I even want to know?"

"Probably not. It involved his hazmat suit's demise and a chess game between him and Tempest. Actually, it was pretty entertaining." Murphy slides to the edge of the couch. "I need a shower. I'm sure I smell something awful. Want me to come back after?"

"I could use a shower too." I stand, pulling him up beside me and toward the bathroom. "Let's save water."

"Shu's right, you did come out of that room bossy." Murphy's voice is flirty. "I like it." He pulls the straps that hold his uniform in place.

"Can I help?" I ask.

"Would anyone in their right mind say no?" His smile is sexy as hell. I push air energy toward him, ripping his training gear off with one blast. Murphy stares at me, wearing only boxers.

"Now, there's a look I've never seen before." I move closer, running my fingers down his chest toward the waistband.

"Are you sure we're ready for this?" He asks.

"I'm definitely ready. You?" With a blink of my eyes, the shower roars to life.

Murphy doesn't answer. He steps closer and slowly

unbuckles the vest of my uniform. It falls to the floor with a thud. "I prefer the old fashion method. Slow and seductive."

"I'm a fan." He moves closer still, leaving less than an inch between our lips. The energy flowing from him melds with mine, igniting a fire inside. I can't get close enough. Our lips meet in a frenzy of movement. The rest of my uniform is off without knowledge of how it happened. Murphy picks me up, our lips never separating, and carries me to the bed.

In a split second, he's on top of me, nothing separating us but thin layers of cotton. Evidence of his arousal touches me, making me want every part of him to touch every part of me. "I love you, Adria." He says, sliding his hand down my side.

"I love you, too," I answer, wrapping my hand around his arousal. He sighs into my mouth at my touch. Slowly, my hand runs the length of him.

"You might want to stop." He sighs as his body shivers. "If not, this isn't going to last much longer."

"We don't want that to happen." I move my hand to his nearest butt cheek, gripping tight. Murphy's thumb skims across my nipple on his way down to the softest part of me. My back arches at his touch. "Oh, gods," I sigh as he slowly slides his fingers inside of me, driving me insane with need. My body's on fire as he pumps his fingers in and out, accelerating with each move. My breath catches in my throat as a coil starts low in my center. His tongue matches the rhythm of his fingers until I can't control the explosion deep inside. My body roars to life as a loud moan escapes my lips. "I want all of you, Murphy."

He slides between my legs, lifting them with his arms. His tongue finds its way to my left nipple while his fingers find its twin. I feel the tip of him pushing into me, asking for permission to enter. My body feels like it's going to explode in anticipation. He makes small movements in and out until the two of us are joined as one. I almost cry out at the fullness of him inside me.

Murphy's movement gets faster as the intensity of our connection grows. The coil starts again, this time more intense than the first. His movements match mine as his breath catches just before the explosion hits me. He pushes into me, refusing to retreat as the two of us cry out in unison.

A red Tiffany lamp in the corner of the room begins flashing uncontrollably. The sink turns on and the toilet flushes repeatedly. The electrical charge in the room matches my energy. Murphy moves his weight to the side of me, still breathing hard. "Gods, that was amazing."

"Agreed," I answer. "Definitely worth the wait."

"Did you turn on the water in the bathroom?" he asks, turning toward the noise.

"I think so. It just kind of happened." I turn the sink and shower off with nothing more than a thought.

He props his head on his hand, running his free hand across my breasts, and down my stomach, drawing crop circles on my abdomen. "You're so beautiful," he whispers.

"So are you." Soft kisses cover my face and neck as we lay together, wrapped in love. "Murphy?"

"Aye?"

"If something happens to me..."

"No, we're not doing that," he interrupts. "We're not putting those vibes into the universe. In fact, we're not going to talk about anything that has to do with war, battles, castles, elementals, or any of it. Tonight's for us, and doing this over and over until someone, most likely Keegan, knocks on the door wondering if we're still alive in here."

I laugh. "I'm pretty sure the entire castle heard that we're still alive."

Hours later, I wake wrapped in the famous Murphy cocoon. I lost count of how many times we devoured each other as if it were our last meal. Soft snores tell me Murphy's still asleep. I slide free, heading toward the bathroom. I needed a shower before, but now I've reached a whole new level of funkiness.

The water in the shower reaches scorch level as I step into the steamy heaven. An audible sigh leaves my lips, loud enough I'd be embarrassed if anyone heard.

"How's it going in there?" Hannah's voice sings over the shower door.

"Hannah?"

"Do you have more than one ghost visiting you while you're in the shower?" Her voice is full of familiar sarcasm.

"Nope, you're the only one."

"So you finally hit it?" Her words are followed by a tiny giggle.

"Hit it? What are you? A seventeen-year-old frat boy named Chad?"

Hannah laughs. "We need to talk." Her tone turns serious.

"Those four words hold so much power." I turn the water off, grabbing the towel hanging on the door. "Give me a minute." I wrap the towel around me but before I can step out, Hannah appears in front of me. Her jeans are dirtier with a few more holes than I remember, and the alien hoodie is faded and worn. Dark circles have taken up residence under her eyes and her cheeks look sunken in. "Are you okay? You look different."

"I'm good. Time passes differently where I am. I guess it's time for a change of clothes." She's lying, but I don't push the issue. "Astrid knows you're planning an attack in a few days."

"Shit," I sit on the edge of the bathtub. "How?"

"I don't know, but she does."

"What does it mean?" I ask, not sure where she's going with this announcement.

She paces the floor in front of me. "It means you have to move up your time and attack today."

I stand, holding my towel in place. "Today? We're not ready. We only hashed out a plan a few hours ago. Today is absurd."

"It has to be today," she answers. "If she comes here, everyone will be slaughtered, including you." She moves inches from my face. "She thinks the attack is in three days. That's the only advantage you have. You're out of time."

"Who are you talking to?" Murphy asks, turning on the mirror light. Hannah's gone.

"I was... I was talking to myself. It's a bad habit I picked up at the compound." I laugh awkwardly. "One of those weird things you do when you're alone."

"What's going on?" he asks. "Adria, please tell me the truth. You're the goddess of fire for gods sake. Nothing you say is going to shock me."

I sit back on the edge of the tub. "I was talking to Hannah."

His forehead wrinkles. "Hannah? Your friend who was killed at the compound?"

"She's been visiting me since she died."

"Visiting?"

"Yes. She tells me things that are going to happen." That sounded crazy leaving my lips.

"Do you see her a lot?" he asks.

"No, just when she needs to warn me about something or talk some sense into me. Look, I know it sounds insane but she's the one who warned me about Earwyn."

"It doesn't sound insane." He moves toward me. "It actually makes sense. I believe you. What did she say this time?"

I sigh, "Astrid knows our plan."

"Shit, she told you that?" He ruffles his hands through his hair, turning his curls into frizz. "The whole plan or just the basics?"

"Basics, I think. Hannah says we have to attack today."

"Today? We're not ready." Murphy echoes my words from earlier, pacing in front of the sink. His sweatpants hang low on his hips, bringing inappropriate thoughts to my mind. "I'll go take a quick shower and let the rest of them know. We'll be ready. Meet you downstairs in an hour?" I nod and watch him walk to the door, praying it's not the last time I see him wear those pants.

......

An hour later, all eight of us, including Brenna, sit around the large table in my office. "Are you sure about this?" Keegan asks.

"Unfortunately, yes. We have to attack today."

"My spies have seen no reason to suspect Astrid knows anything about our plan." Shu stands from his chair.

"Mine either," Llyr adds. "What makes you so sure?"

Tempest stands. "With all due respect, Your Highnesses," he bows to Shu and Llyr. "If Adria says we attack today, then we attack today." He sits back in his seat, crossing his arms in front of his chest.

"Thank you, Tempest." I look each of the members of our makeshift group in the eyes. "I don't want to believe it either, but it's true. We're out of time. If we give her time to attack, we'll die."

"Adria, please don't take this the wrong way. But you've been a First Elemental for all of five minutes. Llyr and I have been Firsts since the beginning of time. We were here before the beginning of time." Shu sits back in his chair. "I believe what my spies say over the imagination of a baby elemental."

I feel the energy rolling off Murphy without looking. He stands from his chair next to me. "How the hell is she *not* supposed to take that the wrong way, Shu?" He moves toward Shu's chair. "What happened to 'you have my full support'? Were those not your words mere days ago?"

"Don't you dare question me, boy." Shu stands,

matching Murphy's energy. "Just because my grand-daughter tolerates you and shares her bed with you, doesn't mean you're on the same level as me. You are nothing more than a hybrid, don't forget your place."

"Shu," Llyr says, standing. "That's enough."

Shu turns toward my father. "Who are you to repri-mand me?" Llyr moves closer to Murphy and Shu. "You've played the role of the human father ever since Adria found her way back to you. We're not human, Llyr. We never have been and never will be." He turns to me. "Adria, I love you. Nothing will change that, but you have to step aside. Llyr and I have experience dealing with situ-ations like this. Astrid is nothing more than a spoiled brat with barely enough sense to match her fall wardrobe." He moves toward a window and away from Llyr and Murphy.

"Llyr, do you feel the same?" I ask.

Llyr sighs, moving back toward his seat. "I question your knowledge of Astrid being aware of our plan, but I don't question you." He pauses, choosing the correct words. "Shu is right. We have millions of years of living this same life, fighting these same battles. Astrid isn't the first to threaten our power and she won't be the last. Sending the lessers in without adequate planning can be more detrimental than helpful."

"You two are suggesting we sit and wait for Astrid to attack us? You heard Adria. We won't survive the attack." Murphy refuses to back down.

I sigh, regulating my thoughts before speaking. "I respect you both and your choices. If you want to leave, leave. But we will attack today. I would rather have my father and grandfather at my side but will not force either of you to choose me over your own beliefs."

Tempest stands. "I will not support your decision to leave, Your Highness. I will stay with Adria." He bows his head to Llyr.

"As do I," Keegan says, moving close to Tempest.

"And I," Brenna says, wrapping her arm around Keegan. Murphy doesn't speak but moves to the other side of Tempest.

"We will do this with or without you, although it would be much easier with you." I join my friends.

Llyr and Shu share a long look, seemingly talking to each other through other methods. "I'm with you." Llyr moves in front of the group. "I won't take the chance of losing you again."

Shu sighs, pops the cork on a bottle of brandy, and drinks straight from the top. "Shit. Don't make me regret this."

CHAPTER 12

"I'm a little pissed at you," Keegan says, as he and Tempest pack their final supplies into packs.

"Why, little man?"

"If there were any time I needed a hazmat suit, this is it."

"You really think that suit would protect you?" Tempest laughs.

"Probably not, but it would make me feel better."

"That's dumb," Brenna adds. "A hazmat suit won't do a bit of good against this kind of fire. Astrid and Adria aren't producing your run-of-the-mill campfire. They're producing fire of the gods. It burns hotter than any fire in our world. You would be dead before you even knew you were on fire."

Keegan stares at her. "You're just a little ray of sunshine, aren't you?" Their banter lightens the mood, and I'm grateful.

"Maybe you could wear one of those fuzzy headbands I've seen you wear. That would protect you about as well as the suit," Tempest says, shoving weapons into his pack.

"That's a sweatband, my giant friend. It may seem useless to someone of your qualifications, but in a tennis match it can make the difference between a game point, or out."

Tempest wrinkles his forehead at Keegan. "I only understood about three words in that sentence."

"That reminds me." Keegan stops packing. "Did anyone else hear those noises last night?" Murphy and I both freeze. "It sounded like some kind of wild animal was running loose through the castle."

"A wild animal, you say?" Brenna wears a huge smile.

"Yes!" Keegan answers. "It sounded like it was growling at one point."

Tempest snorts out a laugh. "I heard something too, but it didn't sound like an animal. What about you Murphy? Did you hear anything strange last night?"

"Aye, I heard a lot of strange noises throughout the night." Murphy's words make Tempest snort even louder.

"I'm glad to hear I wasn't the only one." Keegan continues packing. "Might be a good idea to get an exterminator out here, Adria."

"Oh, my gods, Keegan. To be so smart, you can be naive at times." Brenna holds back a laugh.

"What?" he asks, completely confused.

"I'll tell you when you're older," Brenna adds.

Keegan makes eye contact with each of us. "Why are you all acting weird?"

"Who's being weird?" Shu asks, walking into the room.

Keegan nods his head in our direction. "Everyone. I mentioned the noises I heard last night, and everyone got weird."

Shu stops moving. "What kind of noises?"

Murphy clears his throat loudly. "Have you heard any news from Grimsgil?"

Shu pours a glass of brandy. "As a matter of fact, yes." He toasts my direction. "Seems you were right. My spies tell me Astrid is planning on attacking here tomorrow." He takes a large gulp. "I owe you an apology, my dear."

"Mine have reported the same." Llyr walks into the room. "The sooner we leave, the better. Murphy, are the troops ready?"

"Aye," he answers. "Everyone has been prepped for what's to come."

"Do we know what's to come?" Brenna asks out loud what everyone is thinking. "Hell, I don't have a clue what's to come."

"I don't think any of us do." I look around the room at my family. "No matter the outcome today, know that I love and appreciate each and every one of you."

Llyr is the first to interrupt the silence. "Adria, I think I speak for everyone when I say no matter what happens, we will fight for you, for us, with everything we have. We may be outnumbered, but we have something they don't." He pauses. "They're fighting for revenge. We're fighting for love."

"Dammit, Llyr, don't make me cry," Brenna says. A knock on the door interrupts our group.

Rhys walks into the room, and behind him are two men I don't recognize. Both tower over Rhys, with brown curly hair and matching skin. "Excuse me, Adria. These men insisted on meeting with you all."

I clear my throat. "With all due respect, gentlemen. I'm not available for a meeting right now. Rhys will reschedule you for another time." Both men drop to one knee.

"We are here to swear our support to Adria Kane, the goddess of fire." The men speak in unison.

Shu moves toward them, his motions reminding me of a cat on the prowl. "Where's your master, Dagda?" I try to control my surprise at his question.

"Dead, your highness." The man on the right answers. "We do not support the one who killed him." Holy shit, these two are earth lessers, and they've just sworn to help us fight the goddess of their own element.

Shu waves his hand, forcing the two men to their feet and several feet into the air. "Do you think we're foolish enough to believe that story? Your new master, Astrid, sent you to your deaths." Both men kick their feet, searching for anything that might help them breathe.

"Rhys, lock them in the prison," Llyr demands.

"Oh, I have a better idea." Shu twists his wrist bringing the men moments from death.

"Stop." My voice is low and precise. Shu ignores my request. "Shu, stop," I repeat. With a lift of my chin, Shu is hit with a blast of wind, lifting him off the ground and releasing his hold on the earth lessers. Both fall to the floor, coughing and wheezing.

"Adria," Shu says, floating to the ground. "These men

are here as spies. If you can't handle watching them die, none of us stand a chance in the battle.

"That may be the case, but I will not watch you murder them in cold blood." The man who spoke earlier manages to stand.

"Your Highness." His words are slow and drawn out. "We brought an army. We're not alone," he says between coughs.

"An army?" Keegan repeats.

The second man stands to his feet. "An army of one thousand earth lessers is awaiting your orders." He gasps for air.

For the first time since I've known him, Shu's lost for words. "Where are they?" Tempest's voice booms through the room.

"Just beyond the village. We didn't dare bring them into your compound." Both men have returned to full height and have regained their composure.

"You've brought an army to join forces with the goddess of fire to fight against the goddess of earth?" I ask, moving closer to the men. Murphy moves with me in an effort of protection. "You do realize how this sounds?"

"Yes, Your Highness. We do."

"I'm guessing you lost a bet or something," Keegan says with a laugh.

"It was our honor." They speak in unison.

Tempest moves beside me. "Take me to them, to your army of one thousand."

"No, I'll go." Shu steps between the lessers and me. "We can fly to the village in a matter of minutes." He turns to the lessers. "If you're lying, you will not survive."

The men nod. "Get our army ready. I'll be back with or without our new friends shortly." Shu escorts the lessers out of the castle, and I catch a glimpse of them lifting off the ground through the window.

"Murphy, you and Tempest prepare our army. Keegan, help Brenna pack the bags." I turn to my father. "Can we talk?" Llyr offers his arm to me and leads me onto the veranda. It's still early in the morning, to be honest, I have no idea what time it is. "Are we doing the right thing?" I ask, taking a deep breath in.

Llyr wraps his hand around mine. "I wish I had the ability to answer that question with certainty, but I don't. This never gets easier. I've been in more battles than I can number, yet each one is more difficult than the last." He turns, leaning on the railing. "Sending people to their possible deaths is not glamorous. As a matter of fact, it sucks." I turn, facing the same way as him. "So to answer your question, yes, we are doing the right thing. Our only choice is to attack. Brigit was a bitch who would risk the lives of her lessers for a moment of glory. From what I've seen of Astrid, she's the same. There's no doubt in my mind she'd risk the lives of every one of her lessers for a moment of revenge."

Out of nowhere, Shu lands on the veranda without the earth lessers. "There are well over one thousand soldiers ready to join our cause."

"They were telling the truth?" Llyr confirms. His voice holding excitement.

"They were," Shu answers. "They'll join our army as we march toward Grimsgil."

I wrap one arm around Shu and one around Llyr. "Thank you both for being here."

"We wouldn't be anywhere else," Llyr says, kissing the top of my head.

"Agreed." Shu offers a side hug. "Let's go kick some fire elemental ass." We walk into the office just as Keegan finishes the last backpack.

"We're ready," he says, handing me one of the packs. The five of us join Murphy and Tempest in the courtyard. Our army stands tall, ready for whatever hell they're about to face.

Rhys walks down the steps into the courtyard. "You are not required to fight this fight, Rhys. I couldn't ask you to go against your own kind."

"With all due respect, Adria. *You* are my kind." He steps beside Brenna, wrapping an arm around her waist. "I will not watch the woman I love leave for battle without me. I have no problem killing those monsters." I nod, understanding.

Turning to the army of lessers ready to die for me, emotions threaten to overwhelm me. "I stand before you today as your goddess. A goddess that holds the power of three elements inside her. We will be successful, but only with your help. Our strength lies in the power of combined elements. None is stronger than the other. We will help through whatever means possible. Beyond the village, an army of earth lessers waits to join us. With them, we will win this battle ending the war before it begins."

To my surprise, the army erupts into cheers and battle cries. "I couldn't have said it better myself," Shu says, patting my shoulder. "Let's get this show on the road. We have a long way to go, and moving an army of this size will be hard to keep hidden."

"We should meet the earth lessers by the time the sun's fully risen and be at Grimsgil by late afternoon," Murphy says, stepping to my side. "The water elementals are going to split off at the village and enter the sea. Air will fly the remaining fifty miles to the castle." Murphy repeats our plan for the hundredth time.

We form a line flanking the front of the army, each of us shoulder to shoulder. Murphy, Tempest, and Keegan are to my right. Shu, Llyr, Brenna, and Rhys are to my left. The army falls into step behind as we begin our march to destiny.

It doesn't take long for the village steeple to come into view. "The earth lessers are on the other side of that hill." Shu points beyond the village.

"I believe this is our stop." We bring the army to a halt at the crossroads just before the village. "We will get them through the tunnel." Llyr steps to the side and half of the army follows his move. "I love you," he says, moving toward the cliff. Tempest follows, leaving Murphy and me, face to face.

"Be safe out there," I whisper.

"You too." He leans down, resting his forehead on mine.

"Okay, fine. Kiss her," Shu announces, turning his back to us. Murphy doesn't waste any time. His lips are on mine in an instant, and the memory of last night brings heat to my cheeks. A small moan escapes me as he deepens the kiss.

"Oh, my gods!" Keegan exclaims. "That's what I heard last night!" He rubs his ears with his hands, trying to flush the aural memory away.

"I love you," he whispers before pulling away.

"I love you, too." I watch as he follows my father and Tempest, along with half of our army, and heads to the cliff overlooking the sea.

"They'll be okay," Shu reassures. "The earth lessers are not much further. Maybe a half mile or so."

I nod and continue walking. We bypass the main part of the village, trying not to draw human attention. "One of your special milkshakes would be amazing right now." From our vantage point, the roof of Brenna's diner is barely visible.

"I'll make your favorite on the way home." She smiles a warm smile. I hope we have that chance.

"Is that smoke?" A cloud of dust sits above the land a few miles ahead.

"I believe that's our army," Shu answers.

For the first time in a while, butterflies take flight in my stomach. The human side of me suffers from impostor syndrome daily, but this brings it to an entirely new level. It's still hard not to see myself as the foster kid from California with a criminal background and no friends or family. Just ahead are over a thousand earth lessers willing to fight for me. It's overwhelming.

We top a small crest, and the entirety of the army comes into view. Some are in element form, but most are moving around, preparing for their march with us. All of them drop to one knee in unison. Each holds what looks like an ancient spear, and from my vantage point, they resemble pictures of Greek soldiers going into battle. "Say something," Shu whispers from my side.

I take a deep breath, unsure of the proper words. Shu gently nudges my elbow with his. "Thank you, my friends," I yell to our audience. "There are no words to describe our gratitude for your willingness to join us in this fight." The army erupts into cheers. I wait for them to settle before continuing. "Your service will not go unrecognized in our effort to overtake those who seek to oppress us." Again, they cheer. "Please take a moment to gather your belongings. There's no time to waste." The men and women below move quickly, following directions. I recognize the two soldiers walking up the hill to meet us as the men Shu nearly murdered earlier.

Both drop to one knee as they approach. "Your Highness, I am Peter, and this is my brother Pierce. It's our honor to serve you."

"Thank you, gentlemen. Please stand." Peter glances sideways at Shu. "Would you join us at the front as we march?"

Pierce smiles, showing remarkably white teeth. "It'd be our honor." We continue our trek toward Grimsgil. Several hours pass in silence as the terrain changes from mostly grass-covered hills to sharp, pointed rocks. Rhys moves to my side.

"The castle isn't much further, just over that ridge." He points toward mountains that gleam in the sunlight and look a million miles away. "We're about as far as we need to go by foot. She will have spies everywhere." I nod, understanding.

I turn to the brothers. "We're going to fly from here."

Both men look confused. "Our air elementals are going to use their ability to fly the fire elementals into the castle grounds. I'm afraid there aren't enough to fly the earth lessers in too."

"That's freaking brilliant," Peter says. "Don't worry about earth. We have other means of traveling." He turns to the lessers. "It's time to dig!" His words are met with a roar. He turns to me with a smile. "Earth lessers can move ten times faster underground than on top."

"Holy shit! I had no idea. So, you can tunnel your way through, all the way to the castle?"

"Yes. We were marching to keep pace with you." The army of earth lessers pull goggles from various pockets of their uniforms and put them on.

"Why do they look like bugs?" Keegan whispers. He's right, they look like subterranean creatures.

"Did you know they could burrow underground?" I ask Shu.

His eyebrows raise. "Honestly, I never had much to do with Dagda or his lessers, so I'm as surprised as you."

"They'll enter the castle from below, we'll come from above, and the water lessers will come from inside." Keegan smiles with his words. "I don't know about you all, but I'm feeling more optimistic than I was a few hours ago."

"Don't get too excited," Shu answers. "Let's get these people in the air." He turns toward the mountain, lifting his arms high above his head. The sky goes from a beautiful blue hue to dark in an instant. "They're here." He smiles.

One at a time, dark clouds come from the sky picking

up groups of three or four fire elementals and lifting them into the sky. It doesn't take long until only a small group remains. "I'll carry Brenna, Rhys, and Keegan. Can you get the remaining four?" Shu doesn't answer, he just swoops them up like they were no more than leaves, blowing in autumn winds. With a thought, I lift into the sky bringing my group with me.

"I'm going to be sick," Keegan says as we follow the group of flying lessers.

"You'll be fine," Brenna says. "Pretend it's one of those roller coasters you're so fond of."

The earth lessers disappear into the ground as our group does the same through the sky.

CHAPTER 13

"The castle isn't much further," Rhys announces as we approach the crest of the mountain. "Be prepared for anything."

"I can see the sea from this height," Keegan says, looking over the mountain peaks.

"Do you see any water lessers?"

He strains to see. "It's hard to tell. Something is moving through the water, but I can't tell exactly what."

"It's them. I can feel their power." Goosebumps cover my skin, sensing the power that's approaching.

"Look below," Brenna points to the ground. "The earth lessers are keeping up with us."

"How are we going to do this? Are we just going to land in the center of the compound, and start killing people, or are we going to try to talk some sense into them?" Keegan asks a question I don't have the answer to.

"I'm open to suggestions," I answer honestly.

"I'm all for landing in the middle and killing anyone or anything that gets in our way," Shu says from in front.

"I second that," Brenna says.

"Shu, why are some of them slowing down?" I notice a few of the air lessers dropping back toward us.

"They appear to be getting tired," he answers. "Adria don't do what I know you're thinking of doing. Don't send them your energy." His voice is softer. "You need every ounce you have for the fight. They'll be fine without it." Dammit, he's right, and that's exactly what I was going to do. "I can see the turrets from here. Your job is getting yourself and the ones you carry there safely." I've never heard Shu sound more like a parent than at this moment, and for once, I don't argue.

I concede to his wishes, moving closer to the front of the group. "When we land, don't do anything until I give the signal." My words carry over the sounds of the wind.

"What exactly will the signal be?" Keegan asks.

"I don't know, but it'll be obvious." The energy grows stronger, the closer we get to the castle. The overload of energy in the air is almost overwhelming. I pull to the front of the group. "It's time." In an instant, each fire elemental loses its human form and morphs into nothing but flames. Fire being carried by the wind. This is what nightmares are born from.

Shu, Keegan, and I are the only human forms remaining. "Keegan, can you shift into flames?"

He smiles and points at his chest. "Hybrid, remember? I can't shift." The thought never occurred to me that Keegan would be in human form, while the rest of us shift into our elements. Maybe he did need his suit.

I return his smile. "Stay close to me." Approaching the castle was not at all like I'd envisioned. There are no monster elementals, no Astrid, no nothing. To the unsuspecting eye, the castle sits abandoned.

"Where are they?" Keegan asks.

"They're here. I can feel them. I'm just not sure where." Shu holds his hand up, stopping our flight. "Adria, what do you feel?"

I reach my energy to all areas of the castle. I feel them too. "I feel them but can't isolate their location. Rhys, is there a place where they could hide?"

Rhys huffs a laugh. "Not when I was here, but that was long ago. Who knows what Brigit did after I left?"

"Shall we?" I ask the god of air.

"We shall. Would you like to lead, or I?"

"I would relish the pleasure," I answer, mimicking his formal tone. I fly my small group into the center of the empty courtyard. We land, followed by Shu and the rest of the air lessers. The groups instantly assume fighting positions. Weapons won't do much good here unless the elemental is severely wounded, either way, each lesser holds a weapon of some sort.

"Our earth friends are here," Shu whispers. I feel them below. Like us, they're waiting in the calm before the storm.

"Adria, can you do that thing you did in the village?" Keegan whispers. I wrinkle my forehead at him. "You know, when you saw the vision of this place and Astrid?"

Maybe I can find where they're hiding. Squatting, I put my hands to the earth. Instantly, I'm met with visions of fire, gnashing teeth, earth lessers other than our own, and Astrid. The image zooms to pictures of long tunnels, deep in the mountains below.

"They're in the tunnels." The words spill from my mouth.

"That's impossible," Rhys says. "Brigit flooded those tunnels years ago."

"It's amazing what you can do when you have subterranean friends," Shu answers.

Shit! Llyr and Murphy are heading straight into her trap. "We have to get to the water lessers before they break through the tunnels."

Rhys turns back to human form. "Adria, if we've made it this far, no doubt they have too."

"No!" I shout, sending Rhys flying with a blast of air. Brenna returns to her form, running to help him. "I'm going to the tunnels," I shout to the group behind me.

Shu flashes in front of me in an instant. He's shifted from a well-dressed businessman to a twenty-foot wall of rushing air. "No. I will not allow you to risk your life. Llyr, Murphy, and Tempest will keep them alive. Your presence will only weaken them."

"Dammit, Shu. Move!" I flick my wrist, pushing into his air. He's clearly affected but doesn't weaken his stance. I push more, and his wall shrinks slightly. "You can't ask me to stay if I can save them!" Keegan steps in front of me.

"He's right, Adria. Hell, Tempest is my best friend, but we have to stick with the plan. You have to be here to fight Astrid. You're the only one who can. If you go into the tunnels, you're going exactly where she wants you."

As painful as it is to think about what could be happening, Shu and Keegan are right. "Shit!" I scream into the emptiness. I send a pulse of energy into the ground where the earth lessers are waiting.

In a matter of seconds, Peter and Pierce are standing in front of me. "Yes, your highness."

"They're in the tunnels. Take your army and run them out, but be careful. The water lessers are in there too. You have to protect them."

"Understood," Pierce says, diving into the ground.

"Astrid!" I call into the wind. Shu has returned to human form and is standing beside me.

"Adria, you're reacting as a human would. You must settle your thoughts and stick to the plan."

"*Well, hello, Adria,*" a sickly sweet voice rings through my mind, followed by a laugh. "*I thought you might come for a visit before too terribly much longer, but I'll admit, I didn't expect you to have so many friends with you. I'm not sure we'll have enough food.*"

I take a deep breath. "*Astrid, show yourself and fight like the First Elementals we are.*"

Her laugh brings anger to my core. "*Now, what would be the fun in that? Right now, I'm quite enjoying the battles going on in my tunnels. I think I even caught a glimpse of your little boy toy earlier.*"

I block Astrid from my thoughts. "She's talking to me." Shu looks confused. "In my head, she's talking to me in my head." His eyes open wide in understanding.

"Keep her talking," he answers.

"They're fighting the water lessers," I announce to anyone listening.

"Our earth lessers will be there shortly, making the

numbers closer to even. We need to draw them to the surface. The fire elementals can't go below," Shu says.

"No, but air can," I answer. Shu smiles, following my thought.

"Yes, they can." He turns to his lessers. With a snap of his finger, half of the air lessers turn into gusts of wind as he leads them to the tunnel entrance. "We'll be right back, my dear." He nods to the fire elementals. "Have them ready for whatever emerges from below." In an instant, they disappear.

"*Astrid, are you there?*"

"*I'm here. Just having a bit of fun with a few fish,*" she answers.

"*Come to the surface.*"

"*Now, why would I do that and miss all this?*"

"*Come to the surface,*" I repeat.

She doesn't answer, and the energy around us shifts. Turning to the fire elementals behind me, I shout. "Be ready! I feel them." Rhys and Brenna have returned to their fire forms and are standing next to me. The ground begins to shake. "Steady!" I shout. "They're coming." In a scene straight from an epic fantasy movie, a hoard of fire and earth flows into the courtyard from all directions. Some are fighting water, air, and earth elements as they surface, while others are running straight toward us.

"Hold!" I yell. What's left of my army follows orders in full attack formation. "Keegan, stay close!" He steps to my side, with a sword drawn and what looks like a medieval knight's helmet over his face. I take a second look. "That's actually smart." He nods in agreement. "Now!" I shout, and the world around me erupts into chaos. With nothing more than a finger twitch, I throw fire monsters through the air, breaking their necks on impact. Keegan stays close, slicing his way through the ones that don't die instantly. I fight the urge to look for Murphy or Llyr. Astrid is my focus. Keegan and I keep up our tag team murder session for what feels like hours.

"Gods, they just keep coming!" Keegan says, swinging his sword. From the corner of my eye, a large earth lesser is plowing his way through the crowd, killing anything that gets in the way. His eyes are clearly focused on me. "Adria?" Keegan warns.

"I see him." Keegan steps beside me, facing the giant heading our way. I send a blast of energy into his core, and he barely stumbles. I repeat the move, hitting him with fire. He stops and roars with the intensity of a lion.

"You just pissed him off," Keegan says.

"He was already that way!" I yell. Together we charge toward the huge man. I send a mixture of fire, water, and air straight at him, knocking him back a few feet. The giant pounds his chest as he roars. I push more energy into the elements, but the man refuses to retreat.

Keegan lowers his sword, combining his fire with mine, pushing the giant even further back. Seconds later, a blast of air from a lesser across the courtyard joins, and with the combination, we're able to push the giant back even further. More and more lessers join in, forcing him to his knees. Out of nowhere, Brenna's fire joins our assault, and the giant's eyes turn white. He's on fire from the inside. I watch in horror as he explodes. Pieces of him fly in every direction, catching several small trees on fire when he lands.

"Bet he doesn't have the guts to do that again," Keegan says, giving me a high five. I nod to Brenna, who returns the gesture.

Keegan and I continue our assault, leaving a sea of monster elementals in our wake. If he's getting tired, he hasn't shown it. "We can't keep doing this!" I yell over the roar of battle. "We're losing too many!" The courtyard is littered with bodies from every element.

"Stop!" Astrid's voice rings from above. Both armies freeze, looking for the source of the voice. "You wanted me. You've got me." Her human form looks just like I remember. Long auburn hair and pale white skin. She's dressed like a low-budget version of Cat Woman, complete with a cape.

Shu appears back at my side. "Dear gods," he whispers. "Who dresses her?"

"Come down here and we can talk, goddess to goddess. Only a coward would hide behind her powers."

Her laugh could rival fingernails on a chalkboard. "You're no goddess. You may have killed my mother and stolen her powers, but you're no goddess."

"If memory serves me right, my dear. You did the same. Does the name Dagda ring a bell?" The earth lessers being led by the brothers' cheer at Shu's words.

"The name does sound familiar. But he was very old and not the smartest." She pauses. "Much like yourself. In fact, after this battle is over, I think I'll pay you and Llyr a little visit."

"You shouldn't tell your enemies your plans. Haven't you watched any horror movies?" Keegan asks, bringing laughs from our army.

"Still an imbecile, I see, Keegan. I'm growing bored with all of you." Astrid reaches behind a pillar, pulling a man toward her. His hands are bound, and there's a bag over his head. "Maybe this will shut you up." She pulls off the bag, revealing my worst fear, Murphy.

A gag fills his mouth, and he's blindfolded. His blindfold is covered in blood, and an open wound covers the right side of his face. Oh, my gods. He's a hybrid, and like Keegan, can't shift forms, making him easy prey. Why didn't I think of that?

"Don't fall for her antics," Shu whispers from beside me. "If she was going to kill him, she'd have done it already. She's using him as leverage. Don't show weakness." His words are nothing more than mindless mumbles behind me.

"Look at the fish I caught in the tunnels." She runs her hands seductively over his chest. Murphy jerks away, anger flows from his energy.

"Adria, don't react," Shu warns again. I close my eyes, praying for answers.

"Let him go," I warn. My voice is low and calm.

"Now, what would be the fun in that?" Astrid asks, wrapping an arm around his waist. Movement from the turret catches my eye. Yellow-blonde hair streaks by, barely visible from below. Tempest? He's in human form.

Keegan steps behind a large stone, moving slowly toward the castle wall. He puts a finger to his lips when I question his movement. "Tell us what to do, your highness," Peter calls to me.

I catch sight of blonde hair again, this time closer to Astrid and Murphy. He doesn't stand a chance against her, neither does Murphy. "Adria," Shu warns from behind. What the hell does he expect me to do? Stand here calmly while she holds Murphy hostage? Hell no, that's not going to happen. With a blink of my eye, my body erupts into flames as I rise above the castle, level with Astrid and Murphy.

"There she is," Astrid says. "That's the bitch I've been waiting for." She pushes Murphy from the top of the turret, and the scene around me moves in slow motion. I watch in horror as he falls helplessly off the wall. I can't think. I can't move. I don't react.

Out of nowhere, a wall of air stops Murphy mid-fall, setting him safely on the ground below. Keegan rushes to his side and cuts his bindings while Murphy rips off the blindfold. I look at my grandfather, not sure what I hope to see. He smiles, nods, and winks. Below me, the battle continues in a clash of water, fire, earth, and air.

"Murphy!" I yell toward the chaos.

"I'm good! Get that bitch!" he yells, joining the fight.

"What a shame," Astrid says, making a clicking sound with her lips. "I was looking forward to seeing him land on the rocks below." Astrid lifts off the ground, matching my fire in intensity. I put all my anger, frustration, and pain and push it straight into her with a blast of pure energy. The intensity knocks her to the ground on the other side of the castle wall.

In the half second it takes me to get to her landing spot, she's gone. "Shit!" I yell.

"Looking for me?" Her whiny voice says from behind. She hits me with a blast similar to mine, knocking me back twenty feet. Astrid moves forward, completely engulfed in flames.

"Astrid, we need to stop this. We can do that, you and I. We can work together to fix this."

"Fix this? What exactly needs to be fixed?" She moves close enough that our flames nearly touch.

"Innocent people are dying." My words are calm.

"Innocent people? My mother was innocent when you killed her. My brother was innocent when you killed him." Her words are followed by a sickly laugh.

"Brigit was anything but innocent. She created monster elementals to feed on humans. There's nothing innocent about that, Astrid."

"Humans are nothing more than stupid meat bags walking around on two legs instead of four. Elementals are gods. Why should I care about humans?" She spits her words.

"Your father was human," I answer. "Did you forget about that?"

"My father was a sperm donor. He was weak, as they all are." She begins to circle me like prey. "I'm growing bored with this conversation. You have something that belongs to me."

"We can both wield the power of fire..."

"Shut up!" she screams, interrupting me. "Fire is mine and mine alone. It belonged to my mother and rightfully belongs to me!" A blast of flames shoots straight at me.

"We can share fire," I repeat, as her flames hit me, joining into my own.

"I don't share!" she yells.

"Join me, Astrid. We can stop the fighting." I reach my hand toward her.

"They're your weakness." She nods toward the battle, raging beyond the destroyed castle wall. "You care too much for them, the lessers." I watch her move closer to the courtyard.

Llyr has emerged from the tunnels, and he and Shu are working as a team, bringing down dozens of the monster elementals at a time. "There's no fairness in our world." She walks through the hole in the wall she left earlier. "Your family lives, while mine is dead."

"I'm out here," I say, following her thought process. "The real threat is me, not

them."

"Yes, they're your weakness." I watch in horror as vines stretch from her hands, shooting straight toward Shu and Llyr. Both gods are caught off guard as the vines wrap around their waists.

"No!" a guttural scream leaves my throat as fire shoots straight into Astrid, burning the vines and freeing my father and grandfather.

She turns back to me, anger flowing from every pore. "Now, why would you do that? I was about to have some fun."

"This fight is between me and you. Leave them out of it. Kill me and the power is yours." Those are the magic words. Her attention returns to me as I lift off the ground using air and fire, leading her away from the castle and the ones I love. Astrid does exactly as I expect. She follows.

I land on the black sand beach where Keegan brought Murphy and me on our first run. Astrid lands facing me.

"I'm bored with this," she announces. "It's time for you to go." Black sand forms an opaque wall between us, blocking her from view. The world around me grows silent as the sand forms the shape of a sword. Slowly, the tip of the sword rotates until pointed at my chest. This feels like a huge game of rock, paper, scissors. What can beat a sword of volcanic rock pointed at your chest? My mind plays through a multitude of possibilities coming up with only one possible defeat, air.

With nothing more than a thought, a large cloud forms in front of me. I imagine the cloud forming into the shape of a shield and watch as it latches onto my arm. Swirling wind, moving faster than I can track, keeps the shield in formation. The sword lunges straight at me, and crashes to the ground, as I block it with my creation.

Astrid doesn't hesitate to form another and repeats the same move from the opposite side. Again, the glass shatters as soon as it makes contact with the shield. "Very good," she says, pissing me off. Her approval is the last thing I need.

Imagining a sword of air to match my shield, I stand, facing her, holding one in each hand. "Thank you?" I answer, jabbing the sword toward her torso. She rolls to the right faster than the air, escaping injury. A newly formed sword of sand is aimed at me again. Astrid forms a shield to match mine. Her sword lunges toward me, somehow stronger, this time not shattering when blocked by my shield.

"I'm looking forward to gaining the power of air." She begins circling me again, her obvious favorite move. "That sword and shield are quite impressive."

"Air is something you'll never gain. Even if you kill me, Shu is the one who holds the power. No matter how much you try to convince yourself that you're stronger than him, you'll never be." Her face changes with my words.

"We'll see about that. He's old and weak. It's time for new blood." She continues circling. "When I'm finished with him, I'll move on to Llyr, giving me the power of all four elements."

"What do you think Brigit was thinking right before she died?" I can't hide the smirk that forms at the look on her face. I struck a nerve. "I'm going to guess she didn't think her life was going to end that day." Astrid reacts just like I hoped. A small patch of stone flies toward me from the cliff we're standing under. I easily block it with my shield. "She was just as arrogant as you are, thinking she was the most powerful creature on the planet. When all along, a weak, clueless, hybrid was stronger than her." Another blast of stones flies at me, easily blocked.

"Shut up!" she shouts. The calm, cool Astrid has been replaced by the real person inside, a spoiled, obnoxious, and confused teenager.

"What about Earwyn? Or Aiden? Or whatever the hell his name was? You should have seen him in prison. He was a complete mess." I keep moving, staying just out of reach.

"You're lying."

I laugh. "His mind was not much more than mush. All those years of abuse under the guise of your mother really screwed him up." A large boulder crashes to the ground behind me. "He kept mumbling, his words didn't make any sense."

"Shut up, bitch!" she shouts as another boulder hits the glass. "You're just trying to upset me."

"I'm telling you the truth. Your mother didn't love you. She raised you to kill the rest of the Firsts and gain their power."

"Exactly," she spits her words. "She wanted me to hold the power."

"Because she controlled you!" I answer, matching her tone and intensity.

Astrid calls on her own power of fire, lifting herself even with the cliff, engulfed in white flame. "Enough of this!" she shouts, as fire rains down on the beach in biblical proportions. I block it with a combination of water and air, but for the first time since coming into my power, I feel my abilities draining. She's strong and pissed, a lethal combination. Black sand joins the assault as my defenses weaken more.

Don't fall for her shit, plays through my mind. Shu's words at the castle. If she defeats me, she and her monsters will kill every human on the planet. I focus all my energy on my shield, pushing her fire back slightly. *I love you*, Murphy's face flashes to mind as he caresses my body. Her fire recedes more.

"What you perceive as a weakness is actually what makes me stronger." I push even harder, ricocheting her fire back to her. Astrid lands with a thud on the beach. She's breathing heavily, but alive. I watch her struggle to stand, her breathing labored. Blood drips from her nose and lip. It's her turn to be the prey as I circle the wounded goddess. "Your weakness came when you suppressed your human side. Your mother taught you that humans were weak and nothing more than food for her monsters. She was wrong. They are far greater than anything you can imagine. There's one thing that Brigit didn't teach you, love. Humans are capable of love in even the bleakest of times. Love conquers all."

Astrid stands tall, regaining her composure. "Brigit loved me."

"That's not love." My words soften. "Love is messy and can hurt like hell sometimes, but what Brigit showed you wasn't love. I feel sorry for you."

She doesn't answer, just straightens her cape. "Whatever, bitch. Tell that to your maker." She shoots another stream of pure energy straight into me, pushing me against the boulders that fell earlier.

"Etach spak dune!" I shout to the sea. Waves crash against the black sand. I raise my hands and repeat the call to arms. "Etach spak dune!" Hundreds of water lessers rise from the bottomless sea.

A gust of wind whispers in my ear, *"Je t'appelle à moi. Repeat the words, my dear."* I recognize Shu's voice, carried in the wind. "Je t'appelle à moi," my words are no louder than a whisper. The sky turns black, and wind lifts the hair off my head in a mass of movement as hundreds of air lessers line the beach, surrounding the two of us. Drawing on the power of the lessers that lend me their strength, I call on fire using words that are already ingrained in my mind. "Eldur!" The words lift me off the ground as a small army of fire lessers join the other elements and stand together to protect me, their goddess.

"You think this scares me?" Astrid asks with a smirk. "Dauða," she shouts as what's left of her horde of monster lessers joins the fight. "You just brought the fight to us," she says, raising her hands above her head.

"No, I brought an army to rid the earth of your filth." I turn to my lessers. "Now!" I shout as water, fire, and air combine their powers ending the fight before it begins. The monster lessers are nothing more than a pile of dust.

"What did you do?" she shouts.

"It's over, Astrid. You will not win this battle or the war." I land on the beach in front of her. The powerful goddess that stood before me minutes ago, is replaced by an anxious teenager. "You have two options." My words are slow and calm. Lessers from each element line the beach behind me.

"No, she doesn't." Llyr's voice startles me as he lands beside me. "I'm sorry to say there can only be one outcome." He puts his hand on my shoulder.

Dammit. "Why?" I turn toward him.

"Because unlike you, she won't keep her word." Shu lands beside my father. "She's immortal, meaning if you let her live, she'll eventually escape. Whether in twenty years, a hundred years, or a millennium, she will escape. And when she does, she will have nothing more on her mind than your death. This has to end today."

"Why do I have to be the one to do it?" I ask, already knowing the answer.

"Because you're the only one who can," Llyr answers.

A combination of elements surrounds Astrid, pushing her back to the cliff wall. In her weakened state, they're able to hold her. The look on her face reminds me of

Earwyn's as he waited for Brigit to save him. She's no more than a child. "I don't know if I can."

Llyr pulls me close, walking me to the shore. "It doesn't have to be today. You've weakened her enough, the lessers will be able to secure her and transport her back to the castle. You'll know when the time is right." His blue eyes mirror mine in intensity and color, as he brushes a loose hair behind my ear. "You did good, kid. I'm proud of you."

"Murphy?" I ask an unspoken question.

"He's fine. He and the boys stayed back to tie up any loose ends with the monsters." I smile knowing Murphy, Tempest, and Keegan have become known as "the boys." "What's left of the monster lessers have been captured and will be executed this evening." This battle turned out better than anyone hoped. We set out to stop Astrid, and that's exactly what we accomplished. I wrap my arms around his waist, relishing his energy. "Let's go home." I nod into his chest. Home sounds amazing.

Movement happens so quickly that I don't have time to process the scene. In a blink of an eye, a mixture of air, water, and fire elementals are thrown in a twenty-foot radius, littering the beach with bodies. Astrid, now free from restraints, moves with a speed that can only be measured by supernatural forces, as she rushes straight into Llyr, ripping his head from his torso.

I watch in horror as his body collapses to the ground in a sickening thud. What the hell? "Llyr?" The world stops. "Llyr!" I shout toward an empty shell of what once was my father. "Oh, my gods! Llyr? Dad! Daddy!" Visions of him holding me as an infant flash through my mind, all memories I didn't know I still carried. He was there, and now he's not. I bend down, picking up his limp hand into mine. This can't be happening. This has to be a dream. "No! Daddy, I just found you." A stray tear wets his sleeve. "I'm not ready to say goodbye." I turn to the source of his death.

Shu, along with a mixture of lessers has her backed against one of the boulders she tossed earlier. She's not trying to fight them off, instead, she smiles. The little bitch is smiling.

"Move!" The voice that comes out of my mouth doesn't sound recognizable as I lower Llyr's hand.

Shu doesn't hesitate, he steps away along with the rest of the lessers. "How does that feel?" she asks. "How did it feel to watch your parent die in front of you?" She pauses. "Now, we're even." She steps toward me. "I'll take that truce you offered. Guess we'll be sharing two elements now."

I don't bother to respond, instead send a blast of pure energy straight into the monster standing in front of me, holding nothing back. When the light leaves, nothing remains where she once stood, not even the darkness she carried inside.

CHAPTER 14

The next few hours are a blur of emotion. The moment Astrid died, I felt the power of earth enter my body, but unlike when I killed Brigit, it isn't debilitating. My mind feels scattered, but I'm not passed out in a several months-long coma. Actually, being in a coma would be good right now. Memories of Llyr's body collapsing on the beach plays on constant repeat through my mind. Even though I've witnessed elementals die over the years, watching my father's life fade from his eyes feels like the first.

Moments after Astrid's death, Shu cradled me in his arms and flew me straight to Castle Grimsgil, handing me to Murphy. I watched with blurry eyes as Shu explained what happened on the beach and saw the pain in Murphy's eyes discovering the god of water is dead. My father is dead.

Murphy and I have been sitting on the edge of the

courtyard ever since. Lessers are constantly asking him questions, and he gives orders like the leader he is, but he never leaves my side. No matter what he's doing, he keeps a hand on my arm or thigh, letting me know he's there. I'm thankful for the reminder.

The sun has set low on the horizon, which means it must be close to midnight. Activity has calmed down, and most of the lessers have left or returned to their homes. A tall man moves in front of me. He looks familiar, but my brain doesn't make the connection. He drops to one knee.

"Goddess," he says. "It is my honor to serve you in whatever capacity you will have me. I pledge my life to you from this day forward." He taps his chest with a fist, reminding me of something I've seen in a movie long ago.

"Now's not the best time, Peter," Murphy suggests. "Her body will be recuperating for a while after becoming the goddess of earth." Peter, that's who he is. Where's his brother? "My condolences on Pierce," Murphy adds. "I didn't have the chance to know him for long, but he fought and died bravely."

Peter looks down, wiping a tear. "Thank you, he was a good man."

"Adria and I would be honored to have you on our team." Murphy shakes Peter's hand. "When everything settles, you can join us at the castle, if you like."

Peter nods. "I'd like that." He bows his head toward me. "Your Highness, until we meet again." I manage to nod in return. My heart aches for him and the loss of his brother. Thinking about his loss brings up the images of Llyr all over again.

Keegan and Tempest make more than a few appearances, pretending to talk to Murphy, but it's obvious they're checking on me. "Want me to carry her?" Tempest asks.

"No, she'll be fine. She just needs time to absorb her new powers," Murphy answers.

"We're not leaving. We'll stay as long as needed," Keegan adds. Both men bow before leaving.

It's just the two of us again. Murphy links his fingers through mine. "I'm here."

My voice won't work to offer a thank you. "Get some rest. I'll be right here." My eyes close on demand, and I'm instantly taken into a world of blackness.

"Wake up, Adria," Hannah's voice calls, no louder than a whisper.

"Hannah? Where are you?" I'm surprised to be able to speak. She appears right in front of me. Instead of her typical ghost uniform of holey jeans and alien hoodie, she's wearing a warrior suit, similar to mine. Her hair is in a high ponytail, and she looks like a beautiful, older version of herself. "What's going on?" I ask, looking her up and down.

"You did it," she answers with a smile.

"I did, but at what cost?" I fight the tears threatening to fall again. "Llyr's gone." The words barely leave my mouth. "He's dead."

"He's gone from your world, but he's okay." She makes a strange move with her arm, opening a window into another world. In front of me are Llyr and Claire, together. They're in the middle of a grassy field, sitting on a large plaid blanket. Sounds of children laughing, water splashing, and distant conversations surround them. I watch them clink champagne glasses together with an awkward laugh and drink the contents without stopping.

"Is this some sort of memory?"

"Yes and no," she answers. "It is a memory but, in this world, time moves differently. What you're seeing as a memory, is really happening for them."

"That was as clear as mud."

She swirls her hand, closing the window. "I know, but it's the best I can do right now."

"I don't know if I can do this without him."

Hannah snaps her fingers and the two of us are transported back to the compound in California. We're in the middle of the training field, while recruits are sparing all around us. None of them are aware of our presence. She points to the corner of the field where a very skinny Hannah and an even more awkward version of me are sparing. I remember this day. It was Hannah's first at the compound and I was mad that I had to work with her. Her skills were weak, and she had no clue how to do much of anything. It took months for her to improve enough for us to be on equal ground. "Goodness, look at us." I laugh at the sight.

"I know!" she answers. "That was before I discovered pizza."

"How did you not know pizza was a thing? Did you grow up in a dungeon or something?" I laugh with my words.

"Not quite a dungeon." She turns me to face her. "But

I didn't grow up human." Any humor I had, drains from my body. I watch as my dead best friend transforms from a petite, young woman into a face I remember from a vision. In front of me stands Vita. The woman who held me while making me watch my mother drown.

I jump off the bench in a startle. Murphy's right where he promised he'd be, sitting not far from where my head was lying. He moves in front of me. "Adria? Are you okay?"

"I don't know," I answer. My body and voice feel normal. Was that real or a dream? I pace back and forth, not sure how to explain something I don't understand.

He stops my movement. "Hey, tell me what happened. Did you see something while you slept? Did you have a vision?"

"Yes, no, maybe. I don't know if it was a dream or my mind playing tricks on me." I look around the empty compound. "Where is everyone?"

He scratches his frizzed-out curls. "Tempest and Keegan are playing some game they created using fire and water." He points toward the castle wall where I see small poofs of fire that are quickly extinguished. "Brenna and Rhys are gathering personal belongings off the bodies to help identify them for their families, and Shu has gone to the Isle of Man to prepare them for what's happened. Everyone else has left." I run toward Brenna and Rhys. Murphy follows without question.

"Your Highness," they both drop to their knees.

"No, we're not doing that. I'm still Adria. I'm still the awkward asshole I've always been. Nothing's changed." I put my hand on Brenna's shoulder. "I just had a dream or a vision or something, and I need your help."

"Of course," she answers. "How can I help?"

"You can tell me what the hell it means." I fill Brenna and Rhys in on Hannah, her death, how we're connected, and how she's visited me for the past year through dreams and visions.

"Let me get this straight," Brenna says. "Hannah comes to you and offers you advice?"

I nod. "In a simplified version, yes."

"Is her advice good? I mean, does she advise you to do things that are harmful to you or someone else?"

I think back over her visits. "No. She's been the driving force behind what's eventually led me here, to this moment."

Brenna sits down on a large rock. "I'm guessing you had a vision or dream of her while you were asleep just now." Murphy and Rhys are as enthralled in this conversation as Brenna is.

I scratch the back of my head. "Yes, but she was different."

"How?" she asks.

"Her clothes and hair were different. She looked clean and mature. She showed me Llyr." Murphy's eyes widen at the mention of his name. "They were together, Llyr and Claire." I wipe a tear at the mental picture. "They were having a picnic in a scene that looked straight out of a romance movie." I pause, not sure how to say the rest without just blurting it out. "There's more."

"What's going on?" Keegan says as he and Tempest join our small group.

Murphy looks at me with question. I nod. "Adria had a dream."

I take a deep breath before continuing. "Hannah turned into Vita." The group stares at me dumbfounded. Brenna is the first to break the silence.

"Vita, the goddess of all, source light herself?"

"Yes," I answer. "The very same one who was responsible for Claire's death."

"What does this mean?" Murphy asks.

"It means she's orchestrated this whole thing from the very beginning of Adria's journey," Brenna answers.

"That's what I don't understand," I continue. "Hannah helped me know what to do when I needed her the most. Honestly, all she did was offer advice or give me a dose of reality. If Hannah and Vita are the same, why would she do that? Why would Vita help me?"

Brenna stands, mimicking my pacing. "Maybe she was setting you up for something."

"That doesn't make sense," Keegan adds. "Also, who's Vita again?"

Tempest speaks for the first time, his voice resonating off the castle walls. "Vita is someone I've only heard about in passing. Are you saying that she's real?"

"She's real alright," Brenna answers.

"I don't know what to say," Tempest admits.

Keegan puts his hand in the air, like a child in grade school. I look at him, wide-eyed. "Who's Vita?" he repeats.

"Vita is the fifth element," Brenna answers.

"There's a fifth element? Water, air, earth, and fire." He counts on his fingers with his words. "What other element is there?"

"Aether," I answer. "Vita is the element of life itself. Pure source energy. She is the element that encompasses all the others."

"But you hold all the elements. Is aether stronger than the combination of all of them?"

"That's the million-dollar question, my boy," Brenna answers. "And one we don't have an answer for."

"Adria's the only one who's seen her and lived to talk about it." Murphy leans his back against the damaged stone wall.

"That's not true," Brenna says. "She's been to Shu's house."

"Why does that not surprise me?" Keegan says.

"Could Shu have had anything to do with all of this?" Murphy asks. "Could he be part of her plan?"

Murphy stands from the wall as Tempest answers. "Shu's been an asshole since I've known him, but he loves Adria. He would never do anything to put her in danger."

"Maybe that means he'd do anything to keep her safe," Rhys speaks for the first time.

"What are you saying?" I ask.

"I don't know what I'm saying, but look around, your highness. Out of the four First Elementals, Shu's the only original left." My stomach drops at his words.

Brenna turns to Rhys. "The only person Shu's concerned about saving is himself. Why do you think he got out of here so quickly?"

"He went back to the Isle of Man after Llyr died," I answer. "That's what Murphy told me." My voice sounds more like a hurt child than a goddess of all elements.

"Aye, that's what he said before he disappeared. I have no reason to doubt him," Murphy confirms.

"I've known Shu for an eternity. He's been a pain in my ass most of the time, but I don't believe he's somehow in cohorts with Vita for some diabolical takeover of the world." Brenna leans against the stone wall. "I watched him with Adria. He's different with her."

"Aye. I noticed that too," Murphy adds.

"Tempest, how fast can you be at the Isle of Man?" I turn toward my first elemental friend.

He stands tall at my words. "In elemental form, a few hours."

I nod. "Good. When you get there, stay hidden. I want to make sure Shu is where he said he'd be." A nervous energy forms in my stomach of sending someone to spy on my grandfather. "Stay in contact with Murphy and Keegan, keep them informed on what you find."

Tempest bows. "My pleasure, your highness." He moves quickly, disappearing into the dusk.

"Rhys, Brenna, go back to the castle of fire and check for any left-over loyalists to Brigit or Astrid. I trust you'll know what to do if necessary."

"Yes, your highness," Rhys responds. The two of them follow the same direction as Tempest leaving Murphy, Keegan, and I alone in the empty courtyard.

"What can I do?" Keegan asks.

"You can help me carry my father home." My words are heavy with emotion. Keegan nods solemnly.

"It would be my honor."

"Where is he?" I ask, leaning into Murphy's side.

"Come, I'll take you to him." He turns to Keegan.

"We'll meet you back here in a few minutes." Keegan nods, understanding this is something I need to do alone. Murphy laces his fingers through mine, leading me into the front of the castle. Unlike the castle Brigit lived in, this one looks straight out of medieval times. The large front door creaks open leading into a dimly lit room. Torches hung on the wall provide the only source of light and cast eerie shadows on the stone walls. He leads me into the first room where a body lays, wrapped in white linens on top of a table.

"Is this him?"

"Aye. Brenna took care of him." The first thing I notice is his head. It's where it should be, held on with fabric.

"She put his head back on." I don't know why that surprises me or even why I mentioned it. I walk to the table, not sure if touching the fabric is appropriate. "He looks so small." Llyr was larger than life. In this dark room, he looks almost human. "I don't feel his energy." Tears stream down my cheeks. "Murphy, I don't feel his energy."

"*You* are his energy. He lives on through you." Murphy gently touches my shoulder.

"Do you think he felt any pain?" I think back to the moment Astrid killed him. The light drained from his eyes instantly.

"From what everyone has said, no, I don't."

"Do you know what the last thing he said was?" I gently rub Llyr's arm as I speak. Murphy shakes his head. "He said I did good, that he was proud of me." I can't hold back the pain. Tears stream out of me in a rush of emotion. Growing up, I called it ugly crying. Standing here, staring at the corpse of my father, that's exactly what I'm doing. I'm ugly crying. Murphy wraps his arms around me, allowing me to cry. "Those are the most ironic words ever spoken. I should've stopped her. I failed him."

Murphy pulls away. "You didn't fail him. What happened was meant to happen. You can't blame yourself. I knew Llyr well enough to say he wouldn't want that for you. He loved you, Adria. More than I've ever seen him love anything in the years I knew him. You don't get to own this guilt. Astrid is the one who killed him, not you." In my heart, I know he's right, but seeing Llyr on this table, so weak and frail, makes me feel different. "Do you want me to step outside so you can say your goodbyes?"

"No," I pause. "I'm not ready to say goodbye." He nods and pulls a makeshift gurney from a nearby room. When did he have a chance to get all this organized?

"I'll meet you outside. Will you ask Keegan to come inside to help me?" I nod, leaving the castle, and find Keegan right where we left him.

"Are you okay?" he asks.

"Truthfully, no. Murphy asked for your help inside." I sit on the bench I slept on earlier.

"Will you be alright out here, alone?"

"I'm the freaking goddess of all elements. If I can't handle being out here on my own for five minutes, then I'm going to have a shitty life." My words are laced with sarcasm.

"Well, that sounded like the Adria we all know and love. Don't do anything dumb while I'm gone. We'll be back quickly."

"Wouldn't dream of it," I answer, putting my head in my hands. True to Keegan's words, they exit the castle, carrying Llyr on the gurney. Knowing how long our walk will be, I use air to lift the three of us, along with Llyr's body off the ground, and we begin the voyage back to the castle of fire.

CHAPTER 15

Thirty minutes later, the castle turrets come into view. I've kept us lower to the ground, and not having to walk saved hours of travel time. No one has spoken since we left, and I'm okay with that. I set us down a few feet from the normally locked front gate, which is standing wide open. "Murphy?"

"Aye. Rhys and Brenna probably left it open. Do you sense anything?" he asks.

I feel around for anything out of the ordinary. Everything feels the same as it did this morning. "No," I don't elaborate as we walk through the entrance.

"Your Highness," Rhys says, opening the front door. I don't bother correcting him. Murphy and Keegan follow me inside.

"Where should we place him?" Murphy asks.

"I don't know," I admit.

"If I may, there's a part of the castle that was traditionally used for wakes and funerals," Rhys says, closing the door behind them.

"No," I shake my head. "I don't want him in one of those abandoned wings. I want him close."

"It's not very far from your quarters," Brenna adds, coming into the room. "It's the wing closest to yours. Brigit remodeled it a few years ago."

I nod and follow the procession upstairs and down the hallway next to mine. It doesn't take long until Brenna opens a set of double doors, leading into a large, open room. The room is a mixture of modern and ancient architecture combined, leaving a strange aesthetic in its wake. A shiny marble fireplace is the main focal point and covers most of the wall ahead. A crystal chandelier casts a mysterious glow throughout the room, as shadows seem to dance along the walls. Dark mahogany wood and plush velvet carpet give the room a strange, comfortable feeling. The only piece of furniture, a large table, sits in the middle of the room. Murphy and Keegan gently place Llyr's body on top of it and remove the makeshift gurney. His body looks so small on top of the massive piece of wood.

"We'll be downstairs if you need us," Brenna says as she and Rhys move toward the door.

"What did you find when you arrived?" I ask before they exit.

Rhys looks down before answering. "There were a few fire lessers when we arrived. None of them were from Astrid's horde. They left on their own without any argument."

"Did you check the entire castle?" Murphy asks.

"Yes. At least the parts that are inhabitable," Brenna

answers. "We found no one." She nods at the table and Llyr's body. "What are your plans for him?"

I take a deep breath before answering. "We will fly him to the Isle of Man tomorrow to be buried on his island." I turn to Murphy. "Can you arrange for Daniel and the jet?"

"Aye." He pulls his phone from his pocket and steps into the hall.

"Keegan?" He looks up at my words. "Please get in touch with Tempest and find out if he's had time to discover Shu's whereabouts yet."

"Yes, ma'am." He moves to the hall, stopping halfway. "If he's a fish or something, can he talk on the phone?"

"Keegan," Brenna warns. His words bring a welcomed smile to my face.

"I'll figure it out," he answers, exiting the room. I look at the two people standing before me.

"If you'll excuse me, I'm going to take a bath." Rhys and Brenna are both covered in dirt, and their eyes are as dreary as mine. "You two get some rest." Putting my hand on Rhys's shoulder. "I appreciate both of you more than you know. We'll figure this out tomorrow."

"Adria?" Rhys calls as I reach for the doorknob. I turn, facing the man I imprisoned less than forty-eight hours ago. "He loved you very much."

"I know." I leave the two of them alone with Llyr. My body feels numb as I stumble into my bedroom suite, peeling off pieces of my uniform one at a time. I don't waste a moment filling the large bathtub with steaming hot water and bubbles. Lowering myself in, I internally beg the water to take the pain of today away.

Against my will, my eyes close, taking me to blackness. "Hello," a familiar voice says. I don't respond. "What's the matter? Now that you're the goddess of air, earth, fire, and water you don't speak to your old friend?" Vita steps in front of me.

"You're not my friend."

Vita instantly changes into the familiar image of Hannah, complete with the holey jeans and alien hoodie. "What about now? Is this better?"

I send a blast of energy toward her, not really sure if powers are a thing in dreams. She moves faster than the fire. "Leave me the hell alone," I warn.

"I can't do that," she answers. With a snap of her fingers, she brings me back to the apartment that Claire and I shared before her death. "We're connected, the two of us."

"Why would you bring me here?" She shrugs her shoulders.

"I don't know. I thought since you were happy when you lived here this memory would cheer you up."

"Cheer me up? You're insane." I move closer to her. "My father died today. An outcome that you've had your hand in since Claire's death. Hell, probably before then. You used me, just like you used everyone to get what you want, whatever the hell it is that you want."

Vita runs her fingers along a picture frame of me sitting in Claire's lap. "The answer is simple. I want to be everything." She disappears.

I wake up to an empty bathroom and cold, bubbleless water. "Are you okay in there?" Murphy says through the closed door.

"I'll be out in a minute."

"I've got your favorite fluffy pj's waiting for you when you're ready."

"That actually sounds amazing. Give me half a minute in that case." Bruises cover my arms and legs, souvenirs from the fight. I mindlessly rub a few of them in the mirror before wrapping the large towel around me. True to his word, Murphy's holding my favorite pj's when I open the door. They're purple and covered with orange unicorns and colorful rainbows. I move straight into his arms needing to feel his energy surround me. He picks me up, carrying me to the bed where he gently dresses me and tucks me under the thick comforter.

"Will you be okay if I take a quick shower? I smell something awful." I nod in response. I watch as he disappears into the shower and returns five minutes later. He crawls into bed beside me wearing a too-small pair of my shorts and shirtless.

"Can you hold me?" I whisper. Without hesitation, he wraps his arms around me, moving as close as possible. His warmth covers me from head to toe. "Thank you," the words barely mumble from my lips.

"You don't have to thank me. I'm here for you and will be here as long as you need." He gently caresses my head. "Get some rest. You need it." My body is exhausted but worrying Vita might make an appearance again makes me anxious.

"You need some rest, too." I kiss him on the cheek. "You were amazing today."

"Not too amazing." He rubs the darkened bruise on

his head. "I'm sorry I wasn't there when... when Llyr died."

"You were exactly where you needed to be. There wasn't anything you could have done to change what happened." A tear falls to my pillow. "I failed him." My words are muffled by tears.

"Don't blame yourself," he answers. "There wasn't..."

"Yes, there was. Don't say what I know you're going to say," I interrupt. "I'm a First Elemental. If anyone could've stopped her, it was me. Instead, I stood there and watched it happen."

"It's easy to look back and see the things you could've done after the fact. But in the moment it happens those choices aren't always there." He wipes a tear from my cheek with his thumb.

"She moved so fast," I remember Astrid's attack. "One minute she was captured by the boulder, the next, Llyr was dead. I didn't even realize what was happening. Llyr was right, I think too much like a human. A First Elemental would've seen that coming."

"Did Llyr see it coming?" he asks, already knowing the answer. "If the strongest First Elemental in existence didn't see her, how would you?" Murphy's phone buzzes on the table next to the bed.

"Is everything okay?" I ask, watching him check the text.

"Keegan talked to Tempest. He said Shu was at the Isle of Man, just like he said." Hearing that Shu told the truth relaxes my worry, slightly.

"Tell Tempest to stay there. We'll meet him tomorrow

when we bring Llyr back to the island." He sends the text before turning back to me.

"Everything's going to be alright." He rubs his hand along my jawbone. "It may not feel like that now, but it will be in the end." He scoots next to me, under the cover. "We both need some rest. I love you, Adria. I was so proud of you tod…" Soft rhythmic breathing takes the place of his words.

"I love you, too." I curl as close as possible. Against all attempts, my eyes close and I fall asleep dreamlessly.

A soft knock on the door wakes both of us. "Excuse me, Adria, Murphy. Daniel called a few minutes ago to say they'd be landing in less than an hour," Rhys calls through the door. "I've taken the liberty of preparing Llyr for travel."

"Thank you, Rhys. Give us a moment." I wipe the drool from my cheek after speaking and turn my pillow so Murphy can't see the wet spot. My foster mother who taught me to meditate used to tell me that morning drool was a sign of a good night's sleep. If that's true, I had the best night's sleep, ever.

"Of course. Breakfast is ready if either of you is hungry," he adds.

Murphy crawls out of bed. In the sunlight, I can see how bad his injuries are. The side of his face is dark with bruises, and one of his eyes is nearly swollen shut. "You're hurt."

"I'll heal. By the time the plane lands, my bruises will be gone. I'm going to take a quick shower and pack a bag. I'll meet you back here in thirty minutes." I nod.

I take a shower, throwing a few items in an overnight

bag. I have no idea how long we'll be in the UK, but clothes are much easier to come by there than in Iceland. If I need something, I can order it. I pack the only dress suit I have, not sure what protocol, if any, will be used for a First Elemental funeral.

True to his word, Murphy's back in my room carrying a backpack in less than thirty minutes. I change into leggings and a hoodie for the flight and stack my hair in a high bun. The Adria in the mirror looks more like the California version than the goddess version. I've missed her.

"Ready?" he asks, taking my bag from me.

"I don't want to see him alone."

Murphy laces his fingers through mine. "We'll go together." We walk down the stairs, side by side.

I'm surprised to see Tempest waiting beside Rhys, Brenna, and Keegan at the bottom of the stairs. "Tempest, I thought Murphy told you to stay at the Isle of Man and wait for us?"

"It was more of a suggestion, really," he answers. "I wanted to be here, with my friends. If there was ever a time to be surrounded by the people we love, it's now."

Keegan turns toward Tempest. "Awe, I love you too, buddy." The look on Tempest's face makes me laugh.

"The car is ready," Rhys announces. "I'll drive you to the airport."

"You're not coming with us?" I ask.

"We feel like our place is here, guarding the castle," Brenna answers for both of them.

"That's probably for the best," Murphy says. I step

toward Brenna, wrapping my arms around her narrow shoulders.

"Thank you," I whisper. "Keep him safe." I nod at Rhys.

"I will," she whispers back. "Keep yourself safe." Rhys opens the door, leading us to a black Suburban I've never seen before.

"Don't tell me there's a garage of cars that I never discovered." I think back to Llyr's garage full of priceless supercars that were destroyed in the fight.

"Brigit didn't have the best style when it came to choosing cars. This is the only one that's not red," Rhys says, opening the back door of the SUV.

"That figures," Keegan adds, crawling into the front seat. Murphy and Tempest slide on either side of me, protecting me from both sides. I feel like a child sitting between her parents. Where a third row of seats normally is, sits a beautiful blue casket. The color reminds me of the sea.

The drive is quiet, as we make our way through the Icelandic countryside. Murphy squeezes my hand as we approach the airport. "They just landed," he says.

"They? Sophie?" He smiles and nods. We park on the runway, next to the *Smith Industries* jet.

"There you are!" Sophie says, running down the stairs toward our SUV. She hugs me tightly. "I missed ya!"

"I missed you too." I hug her back. She pulls away and the two of us watch as Keegan and Tempest load Llyr's coffin into the back of the jet.

"I'm so sorry, Adria. Llyr was a wonderful man." I nod and follow her into the jet.

"Good morning, ladies and gentlemen. This is Daniel, your captain speaking. Please make sure your seatbelts are securely fastened as we begin our flight to the Isle of Man." We follow directions, filling each seat of the small jet. Tempest barely fits in the human-sized seat and grumbles under his breath.

"I hate flying," Keegan says as the plane lifts into the sky. He's sitting next to Tempest and neither fits in the seat very well.

"It won't take long to get there," Sophie says to him. "Maybe if I get you something to eat, it'll be easier."

"I'd like that," Murphy answers. "I'm hungry."

"Why does that not surprise me?" She kicks him on the knee before disappearing toward the back of the plane the minute the seatbelt light beeps off.

"Who's that?" Keegan asks after she disappeared. "She's feisty."

"Her name is Sophie," I answer. "She's great."

"She's kind of hot." He wiggles his eyebrows.

"She's my sister." Murphy's words make Tempest snort a laugh.

"You best leave that one alone. She'll tear you up and leave nothing in return, little man," Tempest answers with a smile.

Sophie returns, carrying a tray of snacks. Keegan smiles awkwardly as she hands him a bag of peanuts and bottled water.

"Sophie, may I introduce you to Keegan Jacobson, my chief of security. He's from Iceland by way of California."

Sophie smiles, repeating his name. "Keegan from California, it's a pleasure to meet you. I'm sorry it's on these terms, but a pleasure, nonetheless."

Murphy sighs as Keegan straightens his shirt. "Hi, I'm Keegan."

Sophie laughs. "I'm glad you cleared that up for me. I was confused." Sarcasm runs deep in her family, and her energy lightens the mood on the plane.

"You're welcome," Keegan answers, oblivious as usual.

CHAPTER 16

The flight is easy, just as Sophie promised. Murphy and Tempest fell asleep as soon as they finished their snacks. Keegan did a horrible job of pretending to read while watching Sophie's every move. I played every game on my iPad, read several magazines, and talked to Sophie whenever she had a moment to sit. Hours have passed, and the plane is beginning to descend. I'm ready to see the shores of my homeland.

"Ladies and gentlemen, we are approaching our destination. Local time is seven forty-five p.m., and the temperature is a comfortable seventy-two degrees. Please fasten your seat belts and secure any loose items." Daniel clicks off the speaker.

"Did you get any sleep?" Murphy asks, stretching his legs in front of him.

"A little," I lie. "I'm nervous."

Murphy laces his fingers through mine, pulling our joined hands to his lips, and kissing the back of my hand.

"Whatever's waiting beyond that door, we'll figure it out together." The wheels touchdown with his words. The plane passes the main terminal, moving to a private area reserved for Dr. Kyler Smith, Llyr's island persona. "Ready?" Murphy stands.

"No," I answer, making my messy bun less messy. "But I don't have a choice."

Sophie moves to the door, sliding the handle open. "That's impressive," Keegan says.

"Thank you," she answers, lowering the stairs. "I learned to open doors at a young age. Some might dare to say I was a prodigy." Tempest snorts a laugh as he and Keegan head toward the cargo area. Waiting below is a black SUV similar to the one we used in Iceland. Stephen, Llyr's butler, is wearing a black suit and hat, looking very much the part of a chauffeur.

Watching Keegan and Tempest slide the casket into the SUV, surrounded by the beauty of the Island, Llyr's home, brings tears to my eyes. Stephen opens the door for me, "Your Highness. It's a pleasure to see you again."

"Thank you, Stephen." We pile into the SUV and begin the short drive to the castle. Passing through the small village, there are no signs of the destruction that happened months earlier. Even the fountain looks like it did the first time I saw it. We pass over the bridge leading to the small island that houses Llyr's castle.

"There you are, my dear," Shu says, opening the SUV door, and offering his hand as an aid. I wrap my arms around his waist instead, burying my head into his chest. Hugging him somehow gives my body permission to release the emotions I've been holding inside most of the day. Tears flow down my cheeks, running straight onto Shu's white sweater. Wrapping his arms around my shoulders, he walks me inside. "I'm so sorry, Adria." We walk to the couch in Llyr's office.

"I should have stopped her." Words fall out of my mouth. "It happened so fast. I let it happen."

Shu doesn't stop my rant as the two of us sit alone in the room Llyr used for centuries. When all my emotions are spent, Shu finally speaks. "Adria, you are no more to blame than me. I was right in front of her. I underestimated her strength and look what happened. Even more than I regret Llyr's death, I regret the pain it's caused you."

I pull away from his grip. "I saw Vita."

"What do you mean, saw her?" he asks.

"I mean, I saw her. After the battle and later at the castle. Both times in a dream."

"How did she look?"

"She looked like my friend," I answer.

Shu pulls away, wrinkling his forehead. "Like in the vision you had of Claire's death? I'm not following this conversation."

"Worse than that. When I was a trainer in California, I had a friend. Her name was Hannah. After she died, she came to me in dreams, or what I thought were dreams." Shu moves toward the brandy cart.

"This story will make more sense with a little brandy." He pours a large glass, propping himself on the edge of the cart, and motions for me to continue. I spend the next ten minutes telling him the entire story of Hannah, of her death and its effect on me, of her visits and conversations, and ending with the revelation of her true identity at Grimsgil.

"Well, shit." He fills another glass. "So, Vita was actually your friend Hannah this entire time?"

"Or Hannah was actually Vita. Either way works."

He takes a sip. "Vita doesn't do anything with a goal. If she put that much time and effort into being someone you trusted, there's a reason."

Her parting words come to mind. "She said she wants to be everything."

He sets his glass down. "Only a child of a First can kill a First. That bitch wanted our powers and made you do the work."

"You're the only original left." My words are soft.

He empties the glass. "That I am."

"What does that mean?" I ask, knowing the answer.

"It means she'll want my powers to add to her collection and you're the only one who can kill me." He crosses his arms across his chest.

"I would never do that," I answer. He toasts the air in front of him. "That doesn't make sense though. If she wants all the elements, why make sure I'm the one to inherit them? I'm now a First which means only a child of a First can kill me. It would be a cycle with no end that benefits her."

"She's no doubt found a loophole."

A knock on the door centers my thoughts back to the reason for being here. "Adria, I've taken the liberty to set your room back to the way it was before the destruction." Stephen stands alone in the large double doors. "Mr. McKenzie is in the room next to yours." The large grandfather clock in the corner of the room strikes nine times.

"Thank you, Stephen."

He nods. "I've placed the casket in the drawing room behind the main staircase. People will want to visit and show their respects for Dr. Smith." The people of this island loved Llyr, even if they didn't know who or what he truly was.

"I believe that's our cue to head to bed," Shu says, finishing his glass. "We'll explore more in a few days." He steps in front of me, pulling me in for one last hug before excusing himself to his room.

"May I walk with you, ma'am?" Stephen asks.

"I'd like that," I say, wrapping my arm through his offered one. "Thank you for everything you've done here. The castle looks better than I remember."

"All in a day's work." He smiles a crooked grin. "I've replaced many of the items in your closet as well. I hope you'll find them to your liking."

"If they're anything like last time, I have no doubt I will," I answer as we top the stairs to the familiar landing. Stephen opens my door and what's inside knocks me back a step. "Oh, Stephen. You've outdone yourself." French doors stand open, overlooking the sea I've missed more than I realized. Before the explosion, my bed was a beautiful wooden, four-poster bed, complete with sheers that lined the sides. The new bed has a fabric headboard covered in turquoise tufted velvet. The colors are perfectly accented by the off-white bedding and deep blue couch on the far wall. Stephen smiles at my reaction.

"You're welcome," he says as I hug him tightly before

he excuses himself. Stepping into the closet, I'm met with clothes that rival what used to be here. I rub my hands along each item, feeling the different textures. This is the first time I've been alone since Llyr's death. A basket of fuzzy blankets sits in the corner of the balcony, just like I remember. I find the twin of my favorite one and wrap it around me as I watch the sun disappear into the sea.

"What if I'm not strong enough?" I whisper to the sea.

"You are," the sea whispers back.

"Tempest, is that you?" I ask, receiving no answer. I wake up hours later, tucked neatly in the new bed and Murphy wrapped protectively around me. His warmth, combined with the feeling of being home, relaxes me from head to toe. Dreamless sleep pulls me back into its welcomed realm.

"Good morning, sunshine," Murphy whispers, caressing my cheek.

"Good morning. Thank you for putting me in bed last night."

He smiles. "You were sound asleep on the balcony when I came in."

"Thank you for everything. I haven't told you that."

"Thanking me isn't necessary," he answers.

"Yes, it is. You've been there every step. I couldn't have done this without you."

"I doubt that. You're the most capable person on this planet." His thumb rubs over mine. "I will be here as long as you need me." Soft kisses caress my forehead.

"What is the protocol for Llyr's funeral?"

Murphy takes a deep breath. "Well, from what I've

read in the very few books that mention a First Elemental funeral, it's up to the First and his beliefs. There isn't a protocol, per se."

"What would Llyr want?"

He scratches his frizzy hair. "I think he would want the village and island people to have an opportunity to see him for the last time, followed by a burial at sea."

"Viking style?"

"Something like that. Maybe instead of shooting an arrow, you can light the boat with your powers. If that's too much, we can arrange..."

"No," I interrupt. "That sounds perfect. Returning him to the sea is a beautiful tribute. One he would appreciate."

"Adria?" Stephen knocks on the door with his words.

"Yes?"

"The villagers will begin arriving at noon. I think you'll find appropriate attire in the closet."

"Thank you, Stephen." Footsteps decrescendo down the hall.

"I'm going to get ready. Will you be okay alone?" Murphy stands, still holding my hand. I nod, enjoying the view as he leaves.

With the amount of makeup Stephen has restocked, I could open my own store. I take my time getting ready without the help of YouTube. Today isn't about me. Pulling my hair back in a low, conservative bun, the Adria staring back in the mirror somehow looks older with a hint of sadness.

Several pantsuits hang next to a few sparkling, floor-length gowns. I choose a black, three-button suit and a

pair of low black heels. Pearl earrings and a matching neck-
lace finish off the ensemble.

Murphy's waiting on the landing, wearing a black suit
very similar to mine. His crisp white shirt is in stark
contrast to the black tie and coat he wears. "You look
beautiful," he says, pulling my hands into his. "Are you
ready?"

"As ready as I can be for something like this," I answer.
"I don't know if anyone is ever ready for the funeral of
their father."

"No, you're probably right." He holds his arm out to
me. "Shall we?" I slide my arm through his and we head
downstairs.

Keegan and Tempest are waiting at the bottom. Both
are dressed in suits similar to Murphy's. "You two cleaned
up well," I say, hoping to lighten the mood. To be honest,
I'm surprised Keegan's not wearing a blue leisure suit and
white patent leather shoes.

"You're not wrong," Keegan answers. His coal-black
hair is the same color as the suit, making his amber eyes
stand out more than usual. "Do you think your sister will
be coming to the visitation?" He asks Murphy.

"Aye," Murphy answers. "She'll be with my parents."
Keegan smiles awkwardly.

"What did I tell you about that one?" Tempest says.
"She was born and raised on this island with a hybrid as a
brother. Tread lightly."

"Agreed," Murphy says. "Tread lightly."

"I thought you might like to see him before the crowd
arrives?" Stephen says, stepping into the foyer. He
motions to the back room. "He's ready for the viewing."

To my surprise, the casket is open, and Llyr looks to be sleeping. "Stephen, he looks perfect. How did you do that?" Llyr's wearing a navy blue suit, striped tie, and button-down shirt. There's no evidence of his head ever being unattached.

"Didn't take much, miss," Stephen answers. "That was the suit he wore the most. I figured it'd be the one he'd want to wear for eternity."

Murphy motions the rest of the crew out. "Why don't we give Adria some time alone?" I watch as they quietly leave the room.

I touch his cheek, surprised by the coolness of his skin. "I miss you. I don't know if I can do any of this." I pause. "I mean, I've got Shu, but you know how he is. You never know what he's going to do. Hell, I won't be surprised if he shows up to the visitation wearing rhinestones." I laugh at my words. "I'm sorry for not trusting you sooner. You were always kind and loving to me, even when I didn't return the gestures." I slide a loose hair behind his ear. "I don't blame you for Claire or my childhood. I don't think I ever told you that, and I'm sorry. You were only trying to protect me. I know that now." I straighten the collar on his shirt. "I love you so very much." Tears stream down my cheeks. "Goodbye, Daddy." I step away from the casket just as Stephen slides a large pocket door into place.

"Your first visitors are here," he says, walking into the room. "Are you ready for them? I can tell them to wait."

Wiping my eye with the back of my hand. "No, I'm good." He turns to the door. "Wait! Do I have mascara smeared everywhere?" Stephen turns, studying my face.

"Not a single smear."

I take a deep breath. "Okay, I'm ready. Please let them in." On Murphy's arm is a round woman, half his height, and I recognize her instantly.

"Oh, Adria, dear. I'm so sorry!" Bonnie rushes me, wrapping her arms around my waist. "If there's anything you need, please let Ethan or me know."

Ethan pats me on the shoulder. "He was an honorable man." Sophie steps beside her dad and wraps her arms around my waist.

"We're here for you," she says.

"I know, thank you all for coming. It means a lot that you would come to visit him." I answer, looking around at Murphy's family. "After the boat pyre, there will be a meal. I'd love for you all to join us."

"We'd like that," Bonnie answers. The family moves to Llyr's side, mumbling about how great he looks while the next villagers come into the room.

The scene plays over at least a hundred times as villagers and water lessers sing their praises of Dr. Kyler Smith. Murphy stands by my side, keeping a hand on my back, offering his strength through our connection. "This is the last group," Stephen says, leading an older woman I recognize from the village into the room. "If you'll excuse me," Stephen interrupts the soft conversation. "It's time to move outside and say our last goodbyes." In a choreographed sequence, Keegan and Tempest close the casket, hiding my father away forever. The two of them carry him out of the room and away from guests. "This way, please," Stephen says, offering me an arm as he leads us through the back doorway, past the seawall to the small beach I once used for training.

Llyr's body has already been placed in a boat that's anchored a few feet from shore. The crowd stops, and I clear my throat. "Words cannot express my gratitude to you all for your attendance today." My words are cut short as Shu walks onto the beach. With all the busyness in the room, I hadn't realized he wasn't here. He's wearing the opposite of his usual attire, dressed in all black. It takes me a minute to realize it's actually him. I smile before continuing. "My father would have been honored you all thought so highly of him. He loved this island and loved the people who live here. This island was his ancestral home for many centuries."

Shu moves next to me. "Adria, I'd like to say a few words if you don't mind." I nod. He pauses before taking a deep breath. "Kyler, or Llyr as I liked to call him, is, or rather *was* my oldest friend. I guess you could say we grew up together." The crowd mumbles. "We were each other's only friends for countless years. Out of the two of us, Llyr was the better man, we both knew that. Over the years he taught me many things. One of which was the true meaning of love." He takes my hand into his. "Llyr loved everyone, and the people surrounding him knew that. Most of all he loved my *goddaughter*, Adria." He squeezes my hand. "He spent many years searching for her. My only regret is I wasn't able to help him find her sooner." Shu pauses, clearing his throat. "Adria's right when she says he loved this island and its people. You were the backbone of his existence. Thank you for showing your support for him today. Llyr was the kind of man we should all strive to be." He kisses me on the forehead.

"Thank you," I mouth over the voices of the crowd. He nods.

Turning back to the crowd. "Please join us as we bid my father farewell in a traditional and ancient boat grave ceremony."

At my words, Keegan cuts the rope holding the boat in place, and it begins to slowly drift from shore. The crowd is full of lesser elementals and humans, so simply lighting the boat on fire with my power is out of the question. A line of seven water lessers, dressed very human, raise their bows in a full ceremonial ritual. I blink my eyes, and the boat engulfs in flames before the arrows reach their target.

The crowd watches in silence as Llyr returns to the sea from which he came.

CHAPTER 17

*M*urphy's family, along with a handful of villagers, stay for the meal. Stephen, as usual, prepared a small feast, none of which I'm hungry for. Keegan manages to sit in the chair next to Sophie, and I watch the two of them make small talk all evening. Sophie smiles at his stories, and I secretly cheer him on.

"Are you okay?" Murphy asks, linking his hand with mine.

I squeeze his fingers. "Yes, just people-watching."

"Are you watching the show across the table? I need to rescue Sophie."

I smile. "I don't think she's in need of rescue. She looks like she's enjoying their conversation." Murphy rolls his eyes. "Keegan's a good guy. She could do much worse." Like he heard my words, Keegan smiles at me, wiggling his eyebrows.

"Are you planning on staying here or returning to Iceland?" Bonnie asks from beside Sophie.

"To be honest, I haven't thought much about it," I admit. "I'm not planning on leaving anytime soon. That'll be something I'll have to figure out when the time comes."

"You have plenty of time, dear. We love having you both here," she answers.

"That reminds me," Ethan adds. "I got a few new books at the bookstore. Some that might interest you." He leans closer to the table and whisper-yells across it. "It's about elementals. Information I've never seen before. You might be interested in them."

"Thank you, I'd enjoy reading them," I answer. The crowd slowly thins as people excuse themselves a few at a time leaving Tempest, Murphy, Keegan, Shu, Sophie, and me alone.

Shu excuses himself to the bar cart while the rest of us clear the table, taking leftovers and dirty dishes to the kitchen despite Stephen's objections. Sophie and I work on dishes while Keegan and Tempest take several loads of trash out.

"It was a beautiful service," Sophie says, handing me a plate to add to the dishwasher.

"It was. Thank you for coming." I look around, "and for helping with all of this."

"You don't have to thank me." Keegan and Tempest come back inside laughing about something. "Tell me about Keegan," she asks, watching the two of them together.

"He's growing on you, huh?" I laugh.

She hands me a bowl. "I don't know, maybe. He's a little awkward."

"That's the understatement of the century." I laugh.

"You're right, he's awkward and has a magical power of saying the wrong thing at the wrong time, but he's honest, and I trust him with my life." I look over to see Tempest holding Keegan in a headlock, rubbing his head with his knuckles. Keegan's fighting back, but Tempest's hold is too strong. "Dear gods. They look like two middle school kids fighting over a Pokémon card."

"Trust him with your life, huh?" she repeats, laughing at their antics.

"I do. Keegan's the type you just have to discover on your own." I close the door of the dishwasher after adding the last plate.

Sophie smiles. "I might just have to do some exploring."

"Don't let your brother hear you say that?"

"Say what?" Murphy says, coming from the dining room.

"I told Adria I didn't think you were as strong as Tempest." Murphy looks up in question.

"Well, he's a full elemental, I'm only a hybrid. I will have to agree with that assessment." Tempest grabs Murphy, wrapping him in a headlock while Keegan cheers them on.

"Gentlemen, if you would please take your wrestling match outside, I would be appreciative," Stephen says, wiping down the counter.

"Yes, gentlemen. Outside." Sophie says, popping a towel in their direction. Laughing on the same day as my father's funeral seems strange, but Llyr wouldn't expect me to sit around feeling sorry for myself. "Do you have any games?" Sophie asks.

"I don't know," I answer truthfully. "I'm not sure Llyr was the game-playing type."

"There's a theater, or at least there was," Murphy adds.

"It's been fully rebuilt and restocked," Stephen answers. "Retreating to the theater sounds like a *fantastic* idea."

"Lead the way." I motion to Murphy. "I haven't watched a movie in years." We follow him down newly constructed hallways. The stonework is a mixture of old and new but looks original to the castle. He leads us through a set of double wooden doors and into a room I had no idea existed. Plush red carpeting covers the walls and floors, reminding me of the castle in Iceland. Three rows of black leather theater chairs are centered behind a screen that covers the entire far wall. A series of narrow speakers line the walls and ceilings, surrounding the entire room. "This is beautiful." I run my hand across the textured walls.

"Aye, 'tis. Looks better than before," Murphy answers.

"Where are the movies?" Keegan asks.

"In here." Murphy leads them into a closet off the main room.

"Oh, my gods!" Keegan exclaims moments later. "You guys should see this. There are more movies in here than I've seen at any store. What are you in the mood for?"

"Something that doesn't require me to think," Sophie answers.

"That doesn't limit our selection," Murphy teases.

"Rude." She calls into the small closet.

"I got it!" Keegan comes out carrying the latest Marvel

movie. "This is kind of fitting, given everyone in this room is kind of a superhero." He freezes after he speaks, staring at Sophie.

"Don't worry, I know what you all are. I grew up living with a water hybrid. I learned at an early age about all of this, all of you." She motions to the rest of us.

"Okay, good. I thought we might have to lock you up to keep our secret." Keegan smiles, making Sophie giggle.

We take our seats as Murphy starts the projector. Keegan sits between Tempest and Sophie, while I curl up next to Murphy, snuggling a fuzzy blanket around the two of us. Less than thirty minutes pass before everyone in the room, except me, is asleep. Sophie has her head on Keegan's shoulder, who has his head on Tempest's shoulder.

"Bunch of lightweights you have here," Vita says, walking out of the movie screen. "Every one of them is out like a light."

"You just interrupted one of my favorite scenes," I retort. "What do you want?"

"We've already discussed that." She sits in the empty seat beside me.

"I don't remember there being much of a discussion."

"Let's not play games, Adria. You have what I want." She faces me, propping her knee in the chair.

"You do know I'm the only one on the planet who can kill you?"

"Why would you want to kill me?" Her arms cross in front of her chest. "I've been your only friend for years. I was there for you when Claire died, I was there for you when you didn't have any friends, straight out of jail if I remember right. Oh, and let's not forget about the time I saved your life, sacrificing my own in your place."

I stand, moving in front of her. "Every moment we've spent together has been a part of your calculated plan to gain the powers of all elements. Every move you've made, every step you've taken has all been a part of your plan. I refuse to be a part of any of this." I shoot a blast of pure energy straight into her, throwing her back to the wall behind her. In an instant, Murphy, Keegan, and Tempest are at my sides.

Vita stands and straightens her clothes. "There is another," she says before blinking out of existence.

"Who the hell was that?" Keegan asks. "I'm guessing by how fast she got out of here, she's not a run-of-the-mill lesser."

"That was Vita," I answer.

"That aether goddess you were talking about?"

"The very same one," Murphy answers. He turns to his sister, "Sophie, I think it might be a good idea for you to go home. It'll be safer there."

"I'll walk her," Keegan volunteers. "If that's okay with you, of course." He turns toward Sophie.

"I'd like that. Let me know if there's anything I can do," she says, before following Keegan out.

"What did Vita say to you?" Tempest asks.

"Not much," I admit. "She said she wanted my powers and what a wonderful friend she was as Hannah."

"What did she mean when she said there was another? Another what?"

"Another child of a First?" Murphy asks, shrugging his shoulders. "That would make sense."

"Do you think Llyr had another child?" I ask.

"No," Tempest answers. "He wouldn't have kept that a secret."

"What about Shu?" I ask.

"Have you met Shu?" Murphy asks, his voice full of sarcasm. "I don't even know how Claire came about."

"Brigit or Dagda?" I ask.

"More likely Dagda than Brigit, but still, I doubt it. You remember the story of Griffin. I don't think he would bring a child into the world, worried he would suffer the same fate as his father," Murphy answers.

"Then what the hell is she talking about?" I move toward the wall, rubbing the sides of my cheeks. "Ethan said he had a new book with information that I would be interested in. Is it too late to go to the bookstore?"

He looks at his watch. "Probably, but we can go first thing tomorrow."

"What are you thinking?" Tempest asks.

"I don't know," I admit. "Let's all get some rest." Walking back into the main part of the castle, I'm surprised to see Shu sitting alone in front of the fireplace, staring into the flames.

I turn to Murphy. "I'll be up in a minute." He nods.

"Feel like company?" I sit next to my grandfather.

"For you, yes. Anyone else, no." He's cradling a glass of brandy in his lap and his legs are crossed at the knees. He's changed out of the black suit, into a more typical white sweater and jeans. He slides his arm around my shoulder. "I'm feeling a little sorry for myself tonight." He takes a slow drink.

"Thank you for what you said at the funeral."

He takes a sip. "Llyr and I had centuries of not speaking to each other, but everything I said was true. He was my friend. We weren't the kind of friends that talked on the phone or shared deep, dark secrets, but he was there when I needed him, and I like to think he knew I was too." He pauses. "For millennia, it was the four of us. Now I'm all that's left. It should be Llyr." His voice is soft. "Llyr should be here, not me."

I pull away from his arm, facing him. "Don't say that. Yes, Llyr was a good man, but so are you."

"No, I'm not," he interrupts. "I've done things, horrible things. I kept you hidden for all those years. Llyr would never have done that."

"You're right, he wouldn't have, but that doesn't mean he should be alive and you de... gone." I can't bring myself to say the word. "You're the only original First Elemental alive and I need you. That will never change."

Shu scoffs. "You're the most powerful elemental on this planet, you don't need me."

"I may not need you for your powers, but I need you as my grandfather. I love you."

Tears form in Shu's eyes. "Not many have ever said that to me and meant it." He rubs his hand along my cheek. "I love you too, Adria." He rubs his eyes. "Oh, my gods, I'm a mess." Standing from the sofa, he sets his glass on the mantel. "Enough pity party. Tell me what Vita wanted."

I stand. "You know she was here?"

He nods. "I felt her the moment she popped in. She can't kill you, so I thought I'd let her have her conversation with you. I hoped maybe she'd reveal something that can help our cause."

He has a good point. "It was much the same, but she did say something that we're going to research tomorrow morning." He raises his eyebrows in question. "She said there was another."

"Another what?" he asks.

"That's what I'm not sure about. Murphy's father has a new book he wants me to read. He said it contains information he's never seen before about elementals. Maybe there will be a clue inside."

"Sounds like a plan," he answers. "I'll meet you on the landing tomorrow morning." He picks up his glass, finishes what's left, and continues staring into the fire.

......

True to his word, Shu's waiting on the landing. He scrunches his eyes in disapproval seeing Murphy and I come from the same room but doesn't mention it. The three of us head down the stairs and out into the crisp morning air. "Gods, I missed this place," I say, smelling the sea and familiar scents of home.

"It does kind of grow on you." Shu keeps step with Murphy and me. "Where's the car?" he asks, looking around.

"We're walking," Murphy answers.

"Walking sounds like a very human thing to do."

I laugh. "Taking time to enjoy our surroundings doesn't have to be a human thing." I pull his hand. "Come on. It'll do you good to get some fresh air."

Shu makes a face but continues walking. It doesn't take long before the village fountain comes into view. "It's just beyond the fountain." Murphy points to the quaint shop from my memory.

"Top of the morning to ya!" Ethan says as we walk in.

"Is he a leprechaun?" Shu asks. I nudge him with my elbow while Murphy hugs his father.

"Good morning, Ethan. We thought we could possibly look at the books you mentioned yesterday."

"Of course!" He moves behind a striped curtain, returning seconds later. "Here they are. I found them online and had them shipped to the island. I've marked a few pages I thought you might find particularly interesting. Let's go upstairs, it'll be more comfortable there." We follow Ethan up the stairs into their dark, academia-filled apartment.

A black cat comes from the living room, moving straight toward Shu. It purrs as it rubs fur on his white jeans. "Well, hello there little one." Shu bends down, picking up the purring animal.

"That cat is the devil incarnate, and no one can pick her up," Ethan says, handing me the books. "You're the first person to attempt it without nearly losing an eye."

"You've got good taste," Shu tells the cat, rubbing her head. "I've always had a fondness for cats."

"The feeling must be mutual," Ethan says.

"Why don't you stay awhile? I've already got breakfast on the stove." Bonnie appears at the kitchen door.

"What do you think, fluffy one? Should we stay for breakfast?" Shu asks his new friend. She purrs, rubbing her chin into his hand. "Looks like we're staying."

We follow Bonnie into the kitchen where the table is already set for all of us. "Morning," Sophie says, flipping bacon in the cast iron skillet.

"How was your walk last night?" Her eyes grow large with my question, as she nudges her head toward her parents.

"Fine," she answers quickly, putting a plate of bacon in the middle of the table. Shu sits at the table, the cat still in his arms.

Our conversation stays light and easy as Murphy eats most of the food and I move mine around on the plate. "Bring those books out to the study and I'll show you what I was talking about." Ethan stands.

I gather a few plates off the table before Bonnie shoos me away from cleaning. "We've got this, dear." She takes the plates from me. "Best get in there. Ethan is worked up about showing you those books."

Shu and his new furry friend are already on the couch when I enter. "Take a look at this." Ethan opens the book to a yellow sticky note. I read through the passage discussing the types of elementals, not finding anything out of the ordinary.

"What am I not seeing?" I ask, reading the highlighted section twice.

"Allow me." Ethan takes the book from my hands, reading the passage aloud.

"I'm sorry, Ethan. I don't know what I'm supposed to hear. Murphy can tell you, I'm horrible with riddles."

Ethan sighs. "In a nutshell, I believe there's a fifth elemental."

Shu sets the cat down. "Yes. Her name is Vita, and she's the source of everything."

Ethan's eyes grow large. "Are you telling me there is a fifth elemental, and you all knew about it?"

"Yes. She's the goddess of aether, the life force for all living things," I answer.

"Holy shit," Ethan exclaims. "I was right."

"Ethan, watch your language. There are children present," Bonnie calls from the kitchen.

"I think they've heard the word shit before, Bonnie." He looks around at the three of us. "Tell me about this Vita."

"There's not much to tell. She's a bitch who was responsible for the death of my daughter, Adria's mother." Shu stands.

"To think, all this time there's been a fifth element." Ethan scratches his head in a move I've seen Murphy imitate hundreds of times.

"She killed Adria's mother," Murphy repeats.

"Don't make her into something she's not," Shu says. "She's vindictive, sneaky, and would rather squash you than speak to you."

"Thank you, Mr. McKenzie, for your research, but we are well aware of Vita." I stand, joining Shu.

"But are you aware of her child?" Shu and I sit back on the couch.

"What child?" Murphy asks.

Ethan scrambles through a few of the books he's holding. "Here it is." He points to a page in a book that looks older than any of the others. "I didn't understand the passage until now." He stands to read. "If Vita's the source, then this has to be about her." Ethan gets lost in thought.

"Dad?" Murphy nudges his father to get to the point.

"The source of all laid with a man and bore a child of her own. A child that would change the future of the world." Ethan reads the passage out loud.

"Do you have any alcohol?" Shu asks, looking around the room.

"Aye," Bonnie answers from the kitchen. "I'll be right there."

"That's what Vita meant when she said there was another. She was talking about her own child." I connect the puzzle pieces.

"That book looks nearly five hundred years old. If she did bear a child that long ago, would they still be alive? Doesn't the child of a First live a normal human life?" Sophie asks. We all look at Shu for the answer.

"Don't look at me." Shu shrugs. "Claire was and will be my only child. Before her, Griffin was the only one I'd met, and he literally turned into his father and became immortal. I don't know what the life span of a human/god offspring is. I don't know if anyone does."

"What you're saying is, her child could still be alive?" Murphy asks.

"I'm saying it's possible," he answers. "If her child is alive, it would answer the question of how she plans to gain Adria's powers."

"No, it doesn't. Only a child of a First can kill a First. If her child kills Adria, they would gain her powers, but she wouldn't be able to kill them because she's not a child of a First." Murphy has a good point.

Shu drinks the glass of wine Bonnie brought him straight down. "There's one tiny clause to that rule." She hands him a second glass. "Thank you, my dear."

"Care to elaborate?" I ask as he drinks his second glass in the same manner.

He sighs before answering. "Only the child of a First can kill a First. That part you all know, but there's more you don't. The First Elemental parent has the power and right to kill their own child. It was a way to keep us protected." He sets the second glass down.

"Vita plans on killing her own child?" I ask, making sure I heard correctly.

"Looks that way," Shu answers.

I watch as Murphy's body language suddenly changes. He stands up straighter than before and his energy feels slightly off. He clears his throat without making eye contact.

CHAPTER 18

*A*fter our conversation, Shu excuses himself, saying he has something he wants to check on, and blips out of the apartment. Sophie joins us on the walk back to the castle, claiming she forgot something last night. Truthfully, I think she wants to see Keegan again. Murphy is unusually quiet as the three of us enter the courtyard.

"Hi!" Keegan says, jogging to meet us. He heads straight for Sophie, and the two of them share an awkward glance. "Find anything interesting?"

"That's an understatement," Murphy says, leaving us in the courtyard.

"What's crawled up his ass?"

"He's had an eventful morning," I answer.

Keegan wrinkles his nose. "Um, that's not information we all need to know about. What you two do on your own time is none of my business. At least I didn't hear this time."

Sophie laughs. "No, ya knit whit. She means he found out some news he doesn't like."

"Do you know where Tempest is?" I ask.

Keegan nods. "He went for a swim. He said he'd be back in an hour or so, which means any minute now."

"Will you two meet me in the office when he returns?" I follow Murphy's path into the castle and find him on the couch in my room. "You good?" His energy feels different than it did before we left.

"Not as good as you, apparently." His words surprise me. Murphy has never been sarcastic, that's my forte. He doesn't sound like himself.

"I'm going to meet with Keegan and Tempest to fill them in on what we uncovered. Why don't you take a nap? We're all tired from everything that's been going on. I'll check on you afterward." He doesn't answer.

Ten minutes later, Keegan and Tempest walk into the office. "Your Highness," Tempest says with a bow.

"I thought we were past all the formalities. Call me Adria." I motion to the chairs in front of me. "Please, have a seat." Tempest is one size too big for the chair, but he toughs it out anyway while I fill them in on our discovery this morning.

In true Keegan style, he repeats everything I say. "So, let me get this straight. Vita has a child. She plans to have you kill Shu, gain his full powers, then her child will kill you, gaining all your powers then she's going to kill her own child to gain their powers?" He turns to Tempest. "This needs to be a soap opera." Tempest wrinkles his forehead. "You know, those shows that come on television in the middle of the day, where everyone is having sex with everyone else, and someone is usually in a coma." He looks at me for reassurance. "Adria, tell me you know what a soap opera is!"

I smile. "A couple of my foster mothers watched a few of them."

He throws his hands to the side. "See, I'm not making this up."

"This opera of soap sounds fascinating," Tempest answers. It's clear from the look on his face he knows what a soap opera is, he just enjoys getting Keegan riled.

"No, dude. It's not an actual opera." He rubs his head. "Never mind, it's not that important." He motions toward me. "Please continue."

"There's nothing else to continue," I answer.

"So what's the plan?" Tempest's voice resonates. "Are we just going to wait for the kid to show up here?"

"Her child isn't a child. The book where Ethan found the information is over five hundred years old." I sit back in the chair.

"A five-hundred-year-old mummy is coming to hunt you down?" Keegan asks.

"Something like that." I smile. "Vita's first plan is for me to kill Shu. I doubt her senior child will be here before then."

"Is that something that might happen?" Tempest asks.

"Kill Shu? Never. And, if I don't kill Shu, I won't gain his powers and her child won't have to kill me. Problem solved."

"I don't think it's going to be that easy," he answers.

"Sure, it is." I stand. "If you'll excuse me, I'm going to

take a nap. Keegan, why don't you go and entertain our guest?"

Keegan smiles a true smile. "That's a brilliant idea. I'll show her a little Jacobson charm."

"So, I'm guessing she won't be staying long?" Tempest teases as the two of them leave the room.

"Not cool, dude. Not cool. You're supposed to be my wingman." I've always heard opposites attract. It must be true. The two of them have become inseparable and couldn't be on more opposite ends of the spectrum.

Murphy's asleep when I enter. The dream he's experiencing must not be unicorns and rainbows. He's tossing and turning, almost falling off the couch. "Stop!" he shouts. I move close to his side.

"Murphy?" I gently shake his shoulder. He tosses again, nearly hitting my leg. "Hey, Murphy. You're having a dream." He sits up, wrapping his hand around my throat. What the hell? I don't want to hurt him, but his fingers are beginning to dig in. "Murphy, stop. It's me!" He pins me down to the floor, lowering his body on top of mine. His hand cuts off the air, making it impossible to breathe. I send a blast of air into him, pushing him off to the side while I sit up, coughing.

"What the hell, Murphy?" I ask between gasps.

He blinks his eyes. "Adria?" He moves away from me, looking around the room. "What happened? Did I... did I hurt you?"

I stand, moving toward the balcony. "You tried. I had to blast you."

"Oh, my gods. Adria, I'm sorry." He runs his hands through messy curls. "I was having a dream."

"I noticed." I rub my neck.

"You shouldn't have let me hurt you." He watches me rub the quickly forming bruises.

"Are you trying to say it's my fault you choked me?" My words are full of anger.

"No, that's not what I meant." He steps toward the bathroom. "You should've blasted me with something."

"I did." He walks toward me. "No," I push him back with air. "You just choked me, Murphy."

He scratches his head, "I was having a dream that something was attacking me, trying to take over my body."

"So you decided to reenact that dream with me?"

"Gods, Adria. I'm sorry. I don't know what happened." He leans against the wall, keeping his distance.

My anger is replaced by concern. "We've all had a hard few days. Why don't you get some rest?"

"Aye, that's a good idea. I'm so sorry."

"In your own room." He nods and leaves without arguing. I lock the door behind him. Several hours pass before I head downstairs to find Keegan, Tempest, and Sophie at the dining table playing a board game.

"Highness," Tempest says. "Care to partner with me so we can show these two where the murder was committed and in which room?"

"Only if I can be Miss Scarlet. *Clue* is one of my favorites." I sit next to my partner.

"These two have cheated for the last three games." He points to Keegan and Sophie.

"Dude! I wouldn't cheat on a board game. Just admit it, you don't know what a conservatory is and spent too much time trying to figure it out, rather than solve the murder." Keegan throws the manila envelope on the board.

"I know what a conservatory is!" Tempest answers.

"What is it?" Keegan challenges.

Tempest clears his throat. "It's a room you are served in."

"He's not wrong," Sophie adds.

"Don't help him," Keegan says. "Roll the dice genius." He hands them to Tempest.

"I believe Miss Scarlet always goes first," Tempest says, handing them to me.

"So now you know the rules." Their banter eases the tension from earlier. I roll an eight, taking me into the study. Looking over my clues, I make a plan.

"I think Professor Plum did it in the study with the wrench." Everyone looks through their cards.

"Seriously? Can no one prove her wrong?" Sophie says, crossing her arms on her chest.

Tempest smiles. "Check the cards." I pull out Professor Plum, the wrench, and the study.

"You had to cheat," Keegan says, throwing his cards on the table. "No one can guess it right on the first try."

"Guess I'm just a genius."

"What's going on?" Murphy's voice is deep as he enters the room. "Are you flirting with my girl?" He walks toward Keegan, who stands.

"No? We were just playing a game."

Sophie stands. "Murphy, what's wrong with you?"

Murphy shoves Keegan, pushing him a few feet back. "Nothing's wrong with me. What's wrong with you?"

"Enough." I stand, stepping between the two. "Seems like you might need another nap. Come with me." We move toward the stairs.

"I don't need another nap. What I need is to get out of this hell hole and away from these losers." He motions toward my game partners.

"Okay, then let's go for a walk." I steer him toward the balcony door. He doesn't protest as we exit the castle. We walk on top of the seawall and away from prying ears. "What was that about?"

"He was flirting with you. It's obvious he wants you."

"No, it's obvious he wants your sister. Keegan is an employee and a friend. Not a love interest."

"Whatever. What about that big guy?"

"Tempest?" I wrinkle my forehead. "He's one of your oldest friends. I'm his queen, not his lover."

"Why was he sitting so close?"

"Okay, I won't listen to any more of this. I don't know what's going on with you, but this is a side of you I don't like. You're not the jealous type. Why would you now choose to be jealous of two of my most loyal supporters who nearly died saving you from Astrid?"

He huffs. "You don't see what I see."

"Then, by all means, fill me in." I cross my arms.

"They both want to rip your clothes off and have their way with you."

"Have their way with me? What are you, a hundred years old?" I move away from him. "I think it's best for you to go home tonight."

"I am home."

"No, to Ethan and Bonnie's home. And I think it's best for Sophie to stay here."

"Whatever," he answers. "I'd just interrupt your plans with the two of them anyway." I don't respond. Instead, for the first time since becoming immortal, I use my powers to blip from existence, leaving Murphy behind and sending me straight to Ethan and Bonnie's apartment.

"Oh, dear!" Bonnie yells as I pop into the living room. She stands from the couch wearing a house dress and slippers. "I would've dressed better if I'd known you were coming."

"You look perfect. I have a question to ask and didn't have time to walk." Bonnie's eyes open wide in anticipation.

"Is it alright for Murphy to stay here tonight?"

She looks surprised. "Of course, dear. You don't need to ask. Is everything okay?"

I sigh. "I think we could use some time away from each other."

"We'll have his room ready." She doesn't ask any more questions.

"Thank you," and I blink from the room and back to the seawall. Murphy has moved to the balcony and sitting on a lounge chair. His long legs are stretched over the edge of the chair, and his hands are propped behind his head.

"Back so soon?"

"Take my hand."

He takes my hand, wrapping his entire hand around mine. His grip feels completely different from usual. He pulls our joined hands in front of his face. "Did you know a high percentage of deaths in couples are caused by their significant others?"

"Don't worry, I'm not going to hurt you," I answer, pulling my hand away.

"I didn't think you would." He smiles. Putting my hand on his shoulder, I blip the two of us back to Bonnie and Ethan.

Bonnie has changed into jeans and a T-shirt and is waiting for us to arrive. "Hello, my boy." She walks toward us. "Your father is working on your room. We're both excited to have you." Murphy doesn't speak, just walks to the room, and closes the door. "Oh, my," Bonnie says. "Seems like someone is having a bad day."

"Keep an eye on him, please. He's not acting himself."

"Of course. Are you hungry?"

"Bonnie, quit trying to feed everyone." Ethan comes into the room.

"It's how I share my love." Her answer makes me smile.

"Find any information about what we discovered in the books?" Ethan asks.

I sigh, "No, but I've been preoccupied." Ethan nods, looking toward Murphy's room. "Please let me know if you need anything." I blink out of existence.

I take my time getting ready for bed. The day passed quickly, despite Murphy's strange behavior. Shu still hasn't returned from wherever he went, and I wish he was here. I don't want to be alone tonight. Llyr would know what to do. He knew Murphy his entire life, he'd be able to help. Maybe that's what's wrong with him. He's missing Llyr. Murphy's never been anything but the picture-perfect boyfriend. Perfect in every way. Why, all of a sudden, is he acting like a narcissistic asshole? It's the opposite of who he is.

The water in the shower is life changing as it rips the emotions of the day out of my soul and washes them down the drain. I find a pair of sleep shorts and a tank top in the closet and crawl into bed. My phone buzzes with a text from Sophie. Instead of staying here, she felt like she could be more helpful at home. I hope that's not something we both regret.

S: *Just checked on Murphy. He's asleep and seems fine. Are you ok?*

A: *Yea, I'm good. Glad he's asleep. Maybe he'll be better tomorrow.*

S: *Mom said he was being a jerk. Worse than the game drama?*

A: *No, about the same. I don't know what's going on with him.*

S: *Keegan's here. He's going to keep an eye on him.*

A: *Kegan's there? In your room? Something you need to tell me? Lol*

Sophie doesn't respond, and I set my phone back on the table just as it buzzes again.

S: *Ha-ha! He's on the couch, in the living room. He said he wanted to make sure Murphy doesn't go postal in the middle of the night. Whatever that means.*

A: *Tell him thank you from me, please. Night.*

S: *Done. Night!*

It doesn't take long to fall asleep. "Adria?" a voice calls from the darkness.

"Shit. Leave me alone, Vita or Hannah, or whomever you are today."

She laughs. "What would be the fun in that?"

"Oh, I don't know. Peace?" The woman I remember from my vision at the beach appears in front of me. She's wearing Hannah's signature hoodie.

"Shu came to visit me today." The hairs on my arm stand at attention at the mention of his name.

"Did you hurt him?" I ask.

"Silly girl. You know I can't hurt him. He did have a lot of questions though. If I could kill him, I probably would have just to get him to shut up." She moves closer. I fight the urge to retreat.

"Where is he?"

She wiggles her hands in front of her. "He left. Probably off doing First Elemental things. Hard to believe he's the only original out of the main four earth elementals that are left."

"Looks like you got what you wanted."

"Not quite, but things are looking up."

I move to the side of her. "What's the point of all this?" I point at the hoodie. "Why did you pretend to be my friend? Why did you help me?"

"We've had this discussion before. Remember, on the beach?" I think back to the vision of her holding me, making me watch as Claire was pulled under water.

"You wanted to set in motion the timeline which we would meet now."

"Bingo!" she says, holding up her hands.

"All of this has been part of your plan. Claire's death, Llyr's death, my childhood... all this? You set me up to be the goddess of fire, air, water, and now earth so you could gain my powers and control everything."

She circles me. "It's much easier to take out one person than four."

"You underestimate me."

"There's where you're wrong. I was your friend, remember? I know your weaknesses and your strengths. I know what makes you angry and what makes you cry yourself to sleep at night. Quite a masterpiece if you look at the big picture."

"I know what your plan is, and it won't happen." I stay a step away from her.

"Oh, please enlighten me on *my* plan. This I'd love to hear."

"I won't kill Shu. No matter what you do to me, I won't be responsible for his death."

"You think pretty highly of yourself, don't you?" She continues her circle. "Why would you think I need *you* to kill him?"

"Because you need me to absorb his power to add to my own. Being his grandchild, I have part of his power within me. You're a greedy bitch who needs every ounce. If you send your child to kill me before I absorb Shu's power, you won't ever have full control over air."

Vita smiles. "My child? Who do you think that might be?"

"I think you know very well who that might be."

"We're done here." Vita blinks from the void, leaving me alone in the darkness.

CHAPTER 19

a rogue sunbeam shining through the balcony windows wakes me to an empty room. I don't want to go downstairs and face questions I don't have answers for. Murphy's not acting like himself, and everyone will expect me to know why. Could something be influencing him? No, that's dumb. He's here, on a heavily warded island. If something was going to influence him, it would've happened while we were in Iceland.

"Adria!" Keegan bangs on the door.

"She's not here."

"This is important." His voice sounds more serious than usual.

"Give me a minute." I slip on a pair of sweatpants, a bra, and a hoodie. Opening the door, I find Keegan wearing the same clothes as yesterday and his hair sticking up on the end. "What's going on?"

"It's Murphy. You need to come with me." I follow him out of the castle, toward the village.

"Are you going to tell me what's going on?" I ask, keeping in step with him.

"Something's wrong with him." He opens the door to the apartment to what looks like a bomb went off. Pictures cover the floor, books, and magazines are scattered throughout the rooms and Bonnie is huddled over Ethan, who's lying on the floor in a pool of blood.

"Oh, my gods. What happened?" I move to Ethan's side. His breathing is labored and he's unconscious. "Did Murphy do this?"

Bonnie turns to me with tears streaming down her cheeks. "He's not my boy. Something's wrong." She continues wiping blood dripping from Ethan's brow.

"Sophie, what happened?" Her arms are hugging her waist and the look on her face mirrors Bonnie's.

"I don't know. I heard the noise from my room. By the time I got here, Dad was on the floor and Murphy was gone."

"Keegan?" I turn to my security chief. "Did you see anything?"

He shakes his head. "I was in the bathroom. When I got out here, Murphy had Ethan backed against the bookshelves. When I called out, he punched Ethan and took off."

"What do you mean he took off?"

"I mean he took off. He ran straight out of the apartment."

I stand from Ethan's side. "Find him. This is a small island. He can't be far."

"I'll go with him." Sophie follows Keegan out of the apartment.

Ethan coughs. "Ethan, dear. Are you alright?" Bonnie helps him sit up. He scoots against the edge of the couch, holding the back of his head.

"I think so. I haven't been hit like that since... well, since never." He lays his head in his hands as Bonnie holds a cloth over his wound.

"I'm sorry to ask you this right now, but can you tell me what happened?"

Ethan pauses. "I'm not exactly sure." He looks around for clues. "I was in the window." He points to the large window seat that overlooks the fountain. "I was reading through the book I showed you yesterday, the one that talked about Vita's child. The next thing I know, Murphy ripped the book from my hand, saying something about blasphemy, and pushed me against the bookshelf. He punched me, and I don't remember anything afterward." He looks at all his books scattered on the floor. "Did Murphy do this?"

"I think so," I answer. "I need to find him. Do you have any idea where he could be on the island? Is there somewhere he liked to hang out or hide when he was a kid?"

"He was such a good boy, Adria. This isn't like him. Something's wrong," Bonnie repeats.

"I know. I need to find him so I can help him."

"Don't hurt him." She moves closer to me.

"I don't plan on it."

"You all said the fifth elemental is the goddess of aether. If she's the goddess of source, she will have powers that we can't comprehend. One of them could be visiting the dream world," Ethan says, sliding onto the couch.

"She does." I don't elaborate. "What are you thinking?"

"What if her child also has the same powers?"

"You think Vita's child is the one that's affecting Murphy?"

"I don't know, but it would make sense." He wipes blood dripping from his lip. "Maybe the child is not only affecting him in the dream world but has found a way to affect him in the waking world as well."

"I need to find him," I repeat. If Ethan's right, Murphy won't have any defenses against her or her crazy offspring. "Where would he go?"

"He always loved to hang out at the beach," Bonnie says.

"That's too obvious. It would be somewhere private, somewhere only he and a few other people would know about." I pace in front of the couch.

"The catacombs," Ethan says. "That's what the tunnels underneath the village are. They're ancient catacombs. He used to like to go down there as a child."

I look up. "How do I get there?"

"What about Sophie and Keegan?" Bonnie asks. "You need someone to go with you."

I turn my hand into a pillar of white flame. "I don't need anyone to go with me. He can't hurt me."

"There's an entrance below the bookshop. Most businesses and homes have one." He stands, wobbling a bit, while Bonnie helps to hold him up. "Follow me." I help him downstairs to the bookshop and follow him through an old wooden door that connects from behind the staircase. "It's down here." He opens a second door that looks even older. We continue down another set of stairs until reaching a dirt floor. The smell of mold fills my sinuses instantly. Ethan knows his way around in the dark and grabs something off the wall. The torch lights the room, casting shadows on the walls. "Help me open it." He flashes a light toward a door that's only four feet tall, at most. Together, we pull it open, revealing complete blackness. "Hold on, I'll get another light."

"No, I think it's better for you to stay here. You're injured and I don't know what he's going to be like when I find him." Ethan looks at me sadly.

"Don't hurt him." His voice is soft.

"I'm trying to save him." He nods as I turn my hand into a torch and walk away.

I follow the tunnel for what feels like a few miles. The dirt doesn't have any recent footprints, which means he didn't come this way. Ethan said there are entrances all over the village. I should've asked for a little more insight into Murphy's favorite place to go down here when he was younger. The walls are made of ancient stone and remind me of the walls in the castle prison before they were destroyed. These catacombs must have been built by the island's first inhabitants. The dirt floor gives way to stone as the walls turn into a more modern texture. I must be moving away from the village center into the newer part of the catacombs. Small pinpricks cover my arms as a loud thump echoes off the walls, seemingly coming from every direction. I don't dare call out. Instead, I move forward, hoping to find the man I love.

The further I go, the more modern the tunnel becomes. Brick has replaced the ancient walls and floors, which look much newer and cleaner than before. A shadow of a light flickers in the distance. I release my flame and follow the source. The closer I get, the larger the flames rise. It has to be Murphy. Who else would be in the pits of hell?

A voice echoes through the tunnel and I freeze. I can't make out the words, but the tone of the voice sounds like Murphy. Who's he talking to? Is someone down here with him? With nothing more than a thought, I use my newfound element of earth to camouflage myself and become one with the walls and floor. My entire body blends into the background surrounding me. I'm hidden in plain sight. Using the power of air, I lift inches above the ground being careful not to make a sound. His voice crescendos the closer I get, allowing me to hear more clearly.

"She won't," echoes through the tunnel. I keep going. Movement to my right surprises me as a tall man crosses the path in front of me. He's wearing what looks like a long trench coat, and a top hat and walks with a slight limp.

"Yes, she will," he says, answering the earlier voice. I move close enough to see Murphy standing against the opposite wall. The tall man steps inches from his face. "She'll come looking for you. When she does, you are to kill her."

Murphy looks up. His eyes are swollen and his hair's a frizzy mess. "I won't hurt Adria. You might as well just kill me. I'll die before I let you hurt her."

"That most certainly can be arranged, and knowing

Mother, you won't survive the day. You don't have a choice, you will kill her," the man says.

"No!" Murphy screams. I watch in horror as the man steps even closer to Murphy and disappears inside his body. What the holy hell did I just witness? Murphy's body language changes in an instant. He stands straight, clears his throat, and wipes the dirt from the sleeve of his shirt.

"You should've let me kill her yesterday. It would've been so easy. She would've been butter in my hands."

"Where would the fun have been in that?" A female voice I recognize instantly as Vita answers. The tall man that just reenacted a scene from *Invasion of the Body Snatchers* is her son, and he's inside Murphy. That's why he's been acting like a complete asshole. Vita blips out of existence, leaving Murphy, or whoever he is, alone in the tunnel.

I can't kill Murphy, and Vita knows that. I stay camouflaged in the background as he walks past, unaware of my presence. I don't wait to see where he's going. I blip out of the tunnels, straight to the castle. Tempest is in the dining room, sitting in front of an entire pan of bacon.

"Adria?" he stands. "What's wrong?"

"Murphy." The castle doors slam open as Keegan and Sophie enter.

"We didn't find him. We looked everywhere I knew to look in the village. We were coming here to get a car so we can check further out," Sophie says, panting.

"Don't bother," I answer. "He's in the tunnels."

"Shit, I should've known that. He used to hide there

when he was a kid." Keegan opens the door, heading back to the village.

"No!" I yell. "There's something we need to discuss." Keegan leans against the door frame with his hands propped on his hips.

"This is going to sound crazy, so you might want to sit down." Keegan and Sophie join Tempest at the table. "Ethan discovered an old book with information that has been hidden for years. There was one line that talked about the goddess of aether having a child."

"Vita has a child?" Tempest asks, filling in the blanks quickly.

"Apparently. And, like Vita, this child has the ability to move through dreams, through the void, and through the veil that separates our world from others."

"You sound like some of those ghost shows I've seen late at night. What does all that mean?" Keegan eats a piece of Tempest's bacon.

"It means that both Vita and her son have powers that are beyond this world and our comprehension. I watched her son step inside of Murphy and take over his body."

Keegan stops chewing. "What?"

"I found Murphy in the tunnel, and he wasn't alone. There was a man with him. He was tall, wore a trench coat, and walked with a limp. I watched as he literally stepped inside of Murphy, taking over his body." Each face stares back at me with the same look of horror. "Vita was there too."

"In the tunnels?" Tempest asks. "Did she know you were there?"

"I don't think so. I hid my energy and camouflaged

myself in the background. It must have worked because neither of them felt me."

"Why would he take over Murphy's body?" Sophie asks.

"Because that's the easiest way to get to Adria," Tempest answers.

"With Vita's son in his body, he'll be able to access Murphy's powers along with his own and being the child of a First..."

"He'll be able to kill you." It's Keegan's turn to fill in the blanks.

"She's using Murphy to kill you?" Sophie asks. "What kind of crazy bitch does something like that?"

"The same kind of crazy bitch who killed my mother over twenty years ago, while I watched to set this whole scenario into motion."

"It'll never work. Her son won't be strong enough to make Murphy hurt you." Keegan looks at each of us. "Murphy can fight him off. Can't he?"

"In order to kill Vita's son, Adria will be forced to kill Murphy." Tempest keeps his voice low. "Your Highness, I'm so sorry."

I wipe a stray tear. "It won't happen. I won't kill Murphy."

"You will if it's his life or yours." Shu pops into the room. "If you're forced to choose who lives or dies, the answer is simple. Murphy must die." Tempest moves toward Shu, who's heading straight to his favorite piece of furniture, the bar cart.

Sophie wipes silent tears, and I deliberately don't make eye contact with her. I send a blast of energy straight into the bottle of brandy Shu's pouring, exploding it on contact. His white sweater is immediately soaked. "If it comes to killing Murphy, my choice is easy. I won't do it."

Shu grabs a new bottle from under the cart and continues pouring without acknowledging the explosion. "This is not the time to be a martyr, Adria. You'll be giving Vita exactly what she's worked for and handing it to her on a golden platter."

"You don't get to pop in here, drink all the alcohol, and tell me what I can or can't do. In case you forgot, I'm the goddess of all four elements. I hold dominion over you and the whole damn planet." Energy pours from my body.

"I haven't forgotten anything, darling." Shu's intensity matches mine. "I know precisely who you are, and I know all about your powers." He wiggles his fingers in a circle around me while holding his glass. "Don't choose now to lose this adorable human side."

"Lose my human side? What are you talking about?"

Shu steps closer, "I mean, humans have the innate ability to think about the big picture. Not to just think about themselves. That's what separates them from us, from the elementals. You're half-human. Llyr was wrong. It's not a weakness, it's your strength. It's what makes you the most powerful living creature in the world today or ever." He gulps his brandy. "Your willingness to sacrifice yourself for Murphy is brave, even worthy of a song or two, but how will that sacrifice save the planet?"

"I won't!" I scream.

"Is saving one hybrid worth the destruction of an entire world? *An entire planet?*" His voice is softer. "Look around you. This castle, this island, these people." He points to my friends. "They'll all be gone once Vita gets your power. Are you willing to sacrifice them all to save him?"

Tears stream down my face. I've never felt more human in my life. Sophie grabs my hand. "It's okay," she whispers through tears of her own. "Shu's right, and I have no doubt Murphy would agree."

Shu sits next to me. "Adria, I've looked for another way, but there is none. I'm sorry you have to make this choice, but there's no other way." He reaches his arm around my shoulders, pulling me toward him.

"I don't know if I can," I whisper.

"I can do it," Tempest says from across the table. "I'll kill him for you."

"You won't be strong enough," Shu answers. "Adria's the only one who can defeat Lucian."

"His name is Lucian?"

Shu nods. "I discovered old stories about him on my quest, but no real information. The book Ethan found is the only written information I could find. Until then, rumors of her having a child were just that, rumors. No one has ever even seen him."

"I have."

"Oh, do tell," Shu answers, taking another drink.

"Nothing much to tell. He was tall, and wore a top hat and a trench coat. I couldn't make out his features."

"Well, he sounds lovely." Shu kisses the top of my head.

"He sounds like the hat man," Sophie answers. "It's the first thing that came to mind when you described him earlier." She looks around the room. "None of you have heard of the hat man? He visits in dreams. Every description is the same. Tall hat, long coat, and walks with a limp." She shrugs, "Maybe it's a human thing."

"I remember hearing about him on a ghost show once. If he's Vita's son, that means that bastard's been entering dreams for centuries," Keegan adds.

Shu moves toward the brandy. "Seems maybe people do know what he looks like. What a creep."

"What if I can kill him while he's not in Murphy's body."

"That would be ideal, but he's not going to leave until his mission is complete." Shu straightens his sweater, attempting to wipe the brown stains away. "You are his mission."

"Then I'll just have to make sure he does."

CHAPTER 20

empest, Keegan, and Sophie go to Bonnie and Ethan's apartment to keep them safe. If Lucian's the kind of asshole I think he is, he'll kill them out of spite. Killing Murphy... I can barely even think of the words, let alone do it. Killing him is something only I can do. Shu's powerful, but not as powerful as me. Besides me, Lucian is the only person on the planet who can kill Shu. I won't risk that happening. Despite Shu's objections, I make him promise to stay safe in the castle.

I change into my training gear. Strapping on the heavy vest provides a familiar comfort. I take my time lacing the black leather boots and pulling my hair high on top of my head. It won't take long to find him. In fact, I won't even have to leave the castle. Stepping onto the balcony, I wrap my favorite fuzzy blanket around me, sit in the chair, and allow the waves to relax me.

As soon as my mind clears, I'm met with the blackness of the void. "Adria! What an honor. You're visiting *me* for a change. If I'd have known you were coming, I would have made tea." Vita motions to the nothingness surrounding her. "Oh, look at you, wearing your training gear. Give me just a minute." She snaps her fingers and turns into Hannah, training gear and all. "There, that's better. To what do I owe the pleasure of your visit?"

"Lucian."

Vita's smile leaves. "Who's that?"

"I would think you'd remember since you named him, but maybe not. Quit playing games with me, Vita. You can't even face me in your own skin. Maybe you're scared to be the real you." She changes back to Vita.

"Is this better?" The playful tone of her voice is gone.

"Not really." My voice is laced with sarcasm. "Tell your boy to get out of Murphy, or I'll kill him."

Vita laughs. "You won't kill him."

"I will if I have to." I keep my voice level, not showing any emotion.

"What makes you think Lucian is 'inside' of Murphy." She uses her fingers as quotation marks.

"Careful, you're looking very human."

"I assure you, I'm anything but human. That's your weakness, not mine." I hit a sore spot.

"That's where we disagree. The human side of me is the best part. It's what makes me better than you."

"Better than me?" Vita laughs again. "I'm the source of light and upper air. I am everything. No one is better than me." I don't respond. I surround myself with all the elements, a mixture of air, earth, fire, and water. "That won't help you," she taunts.

I picture the tunnel and the tall man that took over

Murphy. I picture Vita's son, Lucian. I'm transported back to that exact moment. My energy is split between the void, here with Vita, and the tunnels with Murphy and Lucian. I move in between Lucian and Murphy, waiting for the perfect moment. Right as Lucian steps forward, I grab him, wrapping him in a bubble of pure energy, and drag him back to the void with me before releasing the elements surrounding me.

"Lucian? What... how did you get here?" Vita asks.

Lucian looks around, confused. "I don't know." His accent is so strong, I barely understand his words. "Why is she here?" he asks, looking back at me.

"I brought you here," I smirk.

"How's that possible?" He looks to Vita for support.

"It's possible because your mother underestimates me." Lucian takes off his hat. His hair falls halfway down his back, with tiny curls at the end. His eyes are so dark, they look black. His cheeks are sunken in and offset with high cheekbones and an overly defined chin. He smiles, revealing long, jagged teeth.

"I've visited you before. When you were young. Do you remember?" His breath reaches me before his words.

"Stay away from Murphy," I warn.

He moves closer to Vita. "I don't think that's part of the plan." He smiles again. "I do remember you. The pain and anger you carried as a child called me to you."

"Don't flatter yourself, Lucian. I don't remember you."

His laugh is deep and strikes a core memory from childhood. "Oh, I think you do. Look, Mother. She remembers me."

"I think you're right, Lucian. She looks nervous."

"You were nothing more than skin and bones. I made sure it stayed that way." He moves closer to his mother.

"What?"

His crooked smile feels familiar and terrifying. "I made sure the people who you lived with were not very," he turns to Vita. "What's the word? Kind. That's it. That's the word I was searching for."

"Do you know how hard it was for me, or I guess how hard it was for Hannah to listen to you drone on and on about your horrible childhood and all the abuse you endured, blah, blah, blah." Her voice raises an octave. "When the entire time Lucian and I were the source of that abuse? Don't you just love the irony?"

"I feel her anger," Lucian says.

"Of course, you do. She's half-human. They're weak. They're all weak. They wear their emotions on their sleeves."

I refuse to take their bait. "Stay away from Murphy."

"Gladly. He's nothing more than a dumb, slab of meat. You're the grand prize." He moves closer. "Can I kill her now?"

"Well, let me think about it... okay," Vita answers. "I'll worry about Shu later."

"What makes you think you can kill me?" I move opposite his steps.

"Because *when* I kill you, then Mother will kill me, and I'll finally be free of this world." His answer surprises me.

"You want to die?"

"It's what I was made to do. This is what I've trained

and worked for my entire life. I am meant to die for her."
He points at Vita.

"You're willing to die so she can have the power of all
elements?" I keep circling.

"It's an honor to die for such a cause." He copies my
movements opposite of me.

"Have you ever seen the movie *Mommy Dearest*?"

"Enough playing, Lucian. Kill her. I'm tired of
hearing her mouth."

Lucian smiles, revealing his teeth. "Are those fangs?" I
ask, trying to distract him.

"Where do you think the legend of vampires comes
from?" He continues his movement.

"I think it comes from a time much earlier than you.
That's one heck of an ego you've got there."

"Like my mother, I'm bored with you." He moves so
fast I barely track him as he bounces off the invisible air
shield I surrounded myself with earlier. "That was
clever."

"Thank you." I continue moving, reinforcing the
shield. "Are you trying to do the body snatcher thing?" He
moves again, this time he's behind me before I register
movement. Like before, he bounces off the shield. "I'm
growing bored with this." I send a blast of energy straight
into his core. He barely budges. I repeat the movement,
using more power than before.

Lucian takes a few steps back with the blast. Shit, he's
stronger than I expected. Seeming to read my mind, he
smiles. "Going to take more than that, girl." He moves
again, faster than I can track, this time knocking me to the
ground, but not breaking through my weakening shield. I

hit him again with a killer blast. He falls to the ground and jumps up immediately.

"Love is her weakness," Vita says, disappearing into the void. I send another blast, this one a mixture of all four elements. It's enough to knock Lucian back twenty feet, disappearing into the darkness.

"Lucian, stop!" I scream into the void. "Vita doesn't love you. She left you here to die!" There's no sound, no movement, no nothing. "Lucian?" I call. Maybe I knocked him out.

A punch hits my back so hard, I fly through the air, landing face-first thirty feet in the distance. My shield is completely defeated.

"She didn't leave me. It's you she left," he taunts. "She'll never leave me."

"Look around. Do you see her anywhere?" I force myself up, breathing hard.

"Yes, I do. Unlike you, I can see through the void. I can see everything that surrounds us. Admit it. You're weak. Give me your powers, and I'll make it fast. I'll make sure you don't suffer longer than a few days."

"Fuck you, Lucy." I send a blast of pure energy toward the sound of his voice. I hear it hit its mark with a loud grunt along with the thud of a body hitting the ground. Lighting my hand on fire, I move in the direction of the thud, finding nothing.

"Looking for me?" His deep voice sends chills up my spine. I turn, kicking him in the gut. He grunts, slumping over. I move closer and repeat the move from the other side. Clearly, he's never had anyone physically fight back before. I move behind him, kicking him in the back and knocking him to the ground. His breathing has picked up as he struggles to get up.

"What's the matter, Lucy? Not enough cardio in your daily routine?" Using my powers, I wrap a bolt of energy around his neck, pulling it tight. He grasps for air, pulling at the invisible energy. He struggles to get up, pulling at the cord. I kick him again, this time in the back, right above his kidney. He grunts loudly, before hitting the floor hard.

"Stop!" Vita's voice echoes through the emptiness.

"Why would I do that?" I say, pulling the cord tighter around Lucian's neck.

"Because he'll die if you don't." I turn to see Murphy standing in front of her. His eyes and mouth are bound by an invisible force, and blood drips from his lip. His hair is a frizzed-out mess, and he's covered in dirt. Wherever he's been, he's been fighting.

Using air, I lift Lucian off the ground until he's floating a few feet in the air. "Looks like we're at a stalemate."

"You'll do everything you can to save this one, all in the name of love," she hisses.

"And you'll do everything you can to save this asshole, all in the name of you're crazy and need him to kill me because you can't." That was a mouthful.

"You know nothing." Her hands are securely placed on Murphy's shoulders.

"Enlighten me, please."

"I won't waste my time with human nonsense." Vita snaps her fingers, and Murphy buckles over in pain, grasping at his neck. "What you do to Lucian, I do to him." I fight to keep the fear building inside of me from showing. She snaps her fingers, and Murphy's eyes open. "I want him to see that you're the reason for this pain."

Murphy's eyes focus on me. He nods, giving me permission to kill Lucian and ending his life in the process. "Vita, it's me you want. Leave him out of it. You know me well enough to know I don't get attached. He was a good time, but I'm done with him. Let Murphy go, and I'll let Lucian go."

"You're right. I know you well enough to know when you're lying." She sniffs the air. "I smell fear. It streams off you." Testing her threat, I pull the cord tighter around Lucian's neck. He gags, nearly impossible for him to breathe. I watch in horror as Murphy does the same. "Care to keep going?" she taunts. I release Lucian, setting him on the ground. He falls on all fours, coughing and choking for air. "There you go. That's the good little human."

"Now release him," I demand.

Vita smiles. "That was far easier than I expected. You are weak. You always have been." Murphy's still floating, hanging by an invisible noose.

"Release him, now," I repeat. Lucian is still gasping for air as the two of us face off for Murphy's life. "Your mistake is thinking you are in control here." Murphy's eyes close and his feet stop kicking. He's out of time.

"Your mistake is not realizing that I am." Vita claps her hands, and the dim light disappears from the void, leaving us in total darkness.

It only takes one second before I create a light only to realize I'm alone. Lucian's gone, leaving nothing more than a few drops of blood where he was. Vita and Murphy are gone. Oh, my gods. She has Murphy.

I pop out of the void straight to Llyr's office and Shu, who's pacing the floor behind the desk. "What's happened?" he says, moving toward me.

"She's got him. She's got Murphy." My words are barely audible.

"We've known that."

"No, she has him. I found them in the void and kicked Lucian's ass. Vita showed up with Murphy and somehow all three disappeared." I fall to my knees. "Shu, I don't know if he's alive, or dead." Images of his still feet flash through my mind.

Shu helps me to the large couch, sitting beside me. "He wouldn't be of any use to her dead. He's alive or she would've left him there as a statement." Gods, I didn't think about that. "Tell me everything." He sits next to me.

"There's nothing much to tell. Lucian's powers were strong. Stronger than anyone I've had to fight. I turned to human tactics and kicked his ass."

"That's my girl." Shu pulls me to his side. "We'll find Murphy."

Tears stream down my cheeks. "I can't do this without him."

"Yes, you can, and yes, you will," Shu answers. "Vita may have won the battle, but she's not going to win the war."

"I don't know where or how to begin looking for him."

"I do," Shu answers.

......

The last week has been a living hell. I've barely slept, been crying uncontrollably, and an all-around mess. Between losing Llyr and now Murphy, my life feels anything but my own. I've spent most of the week returning to the void, the last place I saw him, finding nothing. No traces of anything or anyone remain. Shu's revelation that he knew where to look has proved unfruitful. There was no trace of any of them at any of her known homes, making this even more difficult.

Sitting on the balcony, I force myself back into the void once again. Just like ten minutes ago, an hour ago, yesterday, and every other time I've tried, it's empty. "Please, Murphy." My words are barely heard through the sobs. "Where are you? I can't find you."

"Why are you waiting for him to find you?" a voice startles me. I look up, surprised to see Claire standing in front of me. She's dressed in a navy blue bathing suit, the same as the day she died, an image straight from my vision.

"Claire?" I ask through tears.

"Yes," she whispers. "I'm here." Memories of Hannah and Vita flash to mind.

"Now you've resorted to pretending to be my dead mother? You really are a crazy bitch."

"Adria, it's me, Claire." She steps closer, reaching a hand to my cheek. I back away just before her skin meets mine.

"Don't," I warn.

She smiles, lowering her hand. "I understand why you don't trust me."

"I expect you do. Where is he? What did you do with him? Is he alive?"

Claire smiles. "I don't know where he is, but I can tell you how to find him."

"Shut up. You and your psychotic son took him. How dare you come back here pretending to be someone who cared about me." Anger overtakes my emotions.

"Adria." Her voice is soft. "I'm not Vita. I know what she did all those years ago. How she separated the two of us, how she set this entire plan into action." Her smile is warm and real. "Search my energy. You'll see that I'm telling the truth."

I do as she suggests and am met with nothing sinister, no lies, only truth, and love. "Mom?" I open my eyes.

"Yes," she answers. "It's really me." She steps closer, wrapping her arms around my shoulders. "My sweet girl. I'm so very proud of you."

Uncontrollable sobs heave from my core. "It really is you. Is he with you?" I look around the void, hoping to find Llyr.

"Your father sends his love. He wasn't strong enough to make the journey with me but wants you to know how much he loves you and to tell you what happened wasn't your fault." She slides loose hair behind her ear, reminding me of my own movement.

"I miss him."

"I know you do. He's growing stronger every day, and we're together," she answers. "He's happy. We're happy."

"I don't know what to do."

"You hold the power inside. Use your gifts, your abilities, and find him." She pulls away, keeping her hands on my cheeks. "Find Murphy."

"How? I've looked everywhere I know to look."

"Trust yourself. Trust your elements. True power comes when they're combined." She backs away slowly. "It's time for me to go. We love you. Never doubt that." I watch as she disappears into nothing.

Finding strength in her words, I do something I've never done before. I focus all my energy on myself, instead of the world around me. I call on the power of earth, feeling the strength fill me, head to toe. I call on the power of air, lifting me off the ground. I call on the power of fire, turning into a human size torch and lastly, I call on the power of water, bringing the love of Llyr in with it. "Show me, Murphy." The words leaving my mouth sound nonhuman and unfamiliar. "Show me, Murphy," I repeat.

The void transforms into something that resembles a dungeon. Ancient stone walls line the small room, and the floors are made of large rocks, worn smooth with age. A small torch provides barely enough light to see further than a few feet. The smell reminds me of the Californian compound. A mixture of blood, sweat, and death. Movement in the corner catches my eye. A rat, the size of a chihuahua, scurries across the floor before being grabbed by something larger. It's not until I share energy with the dim torch, lighting the room completely, that I realize what it is, or more importantly who it is.

"Damn rat," Murphy says. His voice is hoarse and deep.

"Murphy!" I run toward him, reaching to touch him.

My hand passes through his shoulder. I try again, finding the same results. "Murphy!" I scream. He doesn't react. "Murphy! I'm here!"

I watch him break the neck of the rat, adding it to a pile of similar-looking creatures. "You won't win," he whispers. "I won't give up." He struggles to stand. "Did you hear me, you bitch! I will not give up! No matter what you do to me or how many times you threaten me, I will not give up!"

He starts coughing, lowering himself back to the floor. Tears flow for both his pain and his strength. "I love you," I whisper, inches from his face. "I will find you. I promise."

"Fire of the Sky" Chapter One is included in the ebook version of this book. Please scroll forward to read what's in store for Adria and Murphy.

ACKNOWLEDGMENTS

A big thank you to my BFF writing buddy, Stephanie! She's always willing to read a chapter, no matter what time of the day I send them her way. Thank you for being the comma queen and my voice of reason. I couldn't do it without you!

Another big thank you to my mom for being my biggest fan. Without your support, I never would've written in the first place.

Thank you, the reader, for taking a chance on an indie author! Without your support, I couldn't do what I love to do. Adria's story came to me in a dream and she bugged me until I wrote her story. I hope you enjoy her personality as much as I do. She turned out to be a badass and I'm so glad she forced me to write about her.

ABOUT THE AUTHOR

Madalyn Rae is the pen name for an author who loves telling a story. As a teacher of tiny humans during the day and author by night, she hopes she's able to draw you into her world of fantasy, make-believe, and love, even for a brief moment.

She lives on the beautiful white, sandy beaches of the Gulf Coast, with her husband and two loyal, yet mildly obnoxious dogs, Whiskey and Tippi. She's the mother of two amazing adult children and a brand new son-in-law.

When not teaching or pretending to write, Madalyn is immersed in the world of music. Whether playing an instrument or singing a song, she is privileged to know that music is the true magic of the universe.

The Elementals Series will be fully released in 2023, followed by "Vampires of New Orleans", a brand new series in 2023-2024.

www.madalynrae.com

ALSO BY MADALYN RAE

The Elementals Series

Birth of the Phoenix-Adria's Novella-Prequel

Phoenix of the Sea- Elementals Book 1

Guardian of the Sea- Murphy's Novella

Ashes of the Wind-Elementals Book 2

Embers of the Flame-Keegan's Novella

Fire of the Sky-Elementals Book 3

Vampires of New Orleans Series

Garden of the Past-Origin Novella Prequel-Fall 2023

Garden of Secret and Shadow-Book 1-Winter 2023

Garden of Lies and Deceit (Working Title)-Book 2-
Early Winter 2024

Garden of Discovery and Love- (Working Title)
Spring 2024

Printed in Great Britain
by Amazon

35959541R00148